TIME'S ARROW

Journey to Eternity

Philip J Bryant

Strategic Book Publishing and Rights Co.

Strategic Book Publishing and Rights Co.
12620 FM 1960, Suite A4-507
Houston, TX 77065
www.sbpra.com

ISBN: 978-1-62212-233-2

This book is dedicated to my father, George F. Bryant.

To

SHAUN

ENJOY THE READ.

P. ʒ̄ ʒ̄

CONTENTS

ACKNOWLEDGMENTS

After years of reading novels by other people, I thought to myself, "I could write like that." After writing many articles in my local newspaper, and then helping a friend with research for his book, I decided to write my first novel and this is the result.

Science fiction has always been my favourite read. As a teenager, the author Brian Aldiss was my first inspiration with such stories as *Space, Time and Nathaniel, Earthworks,* and the *Airs of Earth,* so I thank him for opening my mind to the most human of conditions: the power of imagination.

I would also like to thank my very good friend and artist, Carol Stewart, who designed and painted the cover to this book, and also her brother Paul who penned the poem 'The Ring' that is shown at the start of this novel.

Finally, I would like to thank my family for believing in me.

Philip J. Bryant

THE RING

Paul Nuttall

Hadrons, leptons, mesons, muons,
Up, down, strange charmed quarks
illuminate the imagination
in beautiful ionized sparks.

Electrons, neutrinos, endless collisions,
exotic particles bloom like a flower,
destroyed and created for curiosities sake
all in the great ring of power.

Acceleration, rotation and ionization,
fission, fusion and light,
the only real limit is imagination,
the answers are almost in sight.

INTRODUCTION

Time, what is time? If you ask someone, they will say it's a minute, an hour, a day or a week, but a minute, hour, a day, or a week of what? The rate of the passage of time is only relative to us here on planet Earth.

We know that time runs at different speeds as you go farther from a gravitational body like the Earth. That's why clocks on satellites have to be continually recalibrated to Earth time. We also know that the faster one goes, the slower time passes. That's why light speed is said to be the ultimate speed barrier, because time gets slower and slower the closer you get to the speed of light, until light speed is attained. So if you were on a space ship that reached light speed, then time would effectively stop for anyone on it.

Why, also does time only travel in one direction, forward? Einstein said that the speed of light could not be surpassed, so time travel could not be possible. However, if a particle was discovered that could travel faster than the speed of light then, according to Einstein's theory of relativity, it would be capable of going backwards or forwards in time.

This could allow for the possibility of time travel. If you look at the night sky on a clear night and look at all those billions of stars, you are looking back in time, as the light that left those stars took hundreds, thousands, or even millions of years to reach us, depending on how far away they are. Some of them may not even exist now, as a star could explode right now, but if that star was say fifty light years away from us, we would not know for another fifty years.

This book attempts to dramatize some of the issues man could face if time travel were really possible and how countries and people might react to having absolute power over time itself.

PROLOGUE

General Sir Stirling Davenport, Joint Chief of the Defence staff, slowly rose and stood looking at all the men and women in the room before delivering his report. He then looked straight at the Prime Minister and said, "I have completed that report you wanted by tomorrow already, sir. Militarily, we have nine Astute-class attack submarines—each carrying sixteen conventional torpedoes—and four Poseidon class SSBN Ballistic submarines with sixteen missiles apiece. Each missile holds a ten-kiloton yield of twelve nuclear warheads, totalling 768 nuclear warheads, enough to effectively wipe out the United States. In summary, we have the capability to totally destroy the United States of America. The American forces have thirty-six attack submarines with twenty conventional torpedoes in each and fourteen SSBN ballistic missile submarines, each with eighteen missiles with sixteen ten-kiloton warheads. This totals 4,232 warheads; that's enough to effectively wipe out the planet, let alone little old blighty! If, for the sake of argument, we happen to know where every single American SSBN sub was at one moment in time—which we don't—and used all nine of our Astute-class attack subs and was lucky enough to sink them. Since they have fourteen, they could still strike Britain with the remaining five SSBN subs using the remaining 1,440 warheads. Never mind the fact that they have thirty-six attack subs out there hunting our nine Astute-class attack subs. In other words, it's oblivion or total oblivion—a no-win scenario—the question is, are the Yanks bluffing? Would they really do it? If they did, then the only country that could stand up against them would be the Chinese, as they now see themselves as the world's policemen, but that would still be no good to us since we're all dead. We could protect our SSBN subs to some extent from the air, but that means carrier protection. We have two super carriers, the Queen Elizabeth and the Prince of Wales, and one aging helicopter carrier, the Ocean. Comparatively, they have eight super-carriers, each of their carriers has more firepower than ours, so basically we're well outmatched. Our carriers would not have subsurface protection because our subs would be hunting theirs, but the Yanks have attack subs to spare, so good-bye three British carriers. At this point, we don't have any attack subs left to sink their carriers so they would still have eight; and then, of course, they still have all their land-based intercontinental ballistic missiles!"

"Thank you General, you've just made my day," replied the Prime Minister. "Has anyone else got anything to add?"

CHAPTER 1

11 hours, 42 minutes earlier:

Monday, 7:45 A.M., Day 1

The alarm clock buzzed in his ear, just as it did every morning. Professor Fenton Jones awoke clutching the pillow next to him. The feeling of loss peaked as he again realized that it had been a dream. Lying there naked, not bothering to turn the alarm off, he let it run the full minute before it turned off. Looking out of the bay window of his small country cottage, he watched the sun slowly rise above the Hampshire hills in the distance. He turned, looking at the empty space next to where he lay for a few moments reminiscing. He remembered her smell, her laugh, and her zest for life. He rose and as he walked to the bathroom he stood looking into the mirror at his thin five foot eight inch frame and partially thinning hair.

"Yep, same old Fenton, just another day," he said to himself.

Just as he said to himself most mornings, except today was not going to be like any other day. Going to the bathroom, he showered, washing the sweat of the night heat from his body, shaved, and dressed, ready for another day at the lab.

* * *

Driving in his open-topped blue Ford Cabriolet usually made him feel free, as if all his worldly worries and cares did not exist. The fifteen minutes it took him to drive to the lab was his favourite part of the day, he thought, as he watched the beautiful rolling green landscape go by. He enjoyed just listening to the birds' early morning chorus as he went, something that had been not possible to hear in the past when people drove around in internal combustion engines. Now that all cars were electric, all you could hear from the car was just the noise of the tires against the road with the wind upon his face. Today though, he could not fully appreciate any of this, as his thoughts were elsewhere.

* * *

Fenton pulled up at the main gates. Martin, the security guard was there to greet him in his usual cheerless manner. "Morning, Mart, another sunny day in paradise," he said as he held up his identification badge.

"Yeah, whatever, Martin grumbled as he pressed the green button that raised the security barrier. No matter what the weather was like, how busy or quiet it was, or how cheerful you were to him, moaning Martin was always the same: grumpy and miserable.

Fenton drove up to his allotted parking slot and backed into the space. Walking swiftly through the main reception area, he acknowledged the receptionist's greeting. "Morning, Professor Jones."

"Morning, Stella."

Stella was about fifty, attractive for her age, with long shoulder length auburn hair, and possessed a cheerful disposition. She was the complete opposite of Martin.

Today was the culmination of almost eleven years of work in designing and building a machine that if it worked would change life here on planet earth, forever. Professor Fenton Jones and his team had built the world's first time machine.

The Particle Atomic Science & Technologies Laboratory, or PASTec, sat in gently rolling hills of the Hampshire countryside. The project was financed by the Ministry of Defence's Special Sciences Department. This department had been established a few years after scientists at the Large Hadron Collider at Geneva in 2011 had discovered a neutrino called a tachyon. They found that tachyons could travel faster than the speed of light, and so according to Einstein's Theory of General Relativity, would have the capability to move forward or backward through time. That was fifteen years ago and seventeen billion pounds later.

Now all that work and money had come down to this day, which is the day that they would attempt to send an item back in time. The previous day, the machine had been turned on and run in neutral for a few hours to test the power systems, all of which was successful. Today it had been decided that the first test would be to send back a digital camera to record that momentous moment at CERN fifteen years earlier and then return it forward in time to the present and see if it recorded. If this was successful, then a live animal would be sent through, and then finally a human. Walking up to his laboratory in the north wing, Fenton held up his identification card to the reader and his eyes were recorded by a retina scanner. After receiving green lights, he finally spoke into a microphone for voice recognition verification. "This is Professor Fenton Jones."

The computer acknowledged him with, "Voice recognition confirmed."

With that, Fenton stepped into a glass pod that closed behind him. After his body was scanned for anything that was not permitted within the laboratory, the glass door then opened in front of him and he stepped through. Even though he had been coming here for almost eleven years, the sight of the time machine never failed to fill him with wonder. To him, it was comparable to a gigantic metal spider. It was an enormous machine at 40 feet wide, 15 feet high and over 28 feet deep. Power cables were connected to it everywhere. They covered the central part of this colossal laboratory. The machine was surrounded by a scaffold on which dozens of technicians feverishly worked, like soldier ants. Right at the centre of this fantastic machine was an opening 10 feet wide, 7 feet deep and 4 feet high. This was the time displacement area, the area where the object, or person, to be sent through time would be placed.

"Morning, prof," said Dylan, the smiling chief technician, "I hear you're hoping to show us some holiday snaps later today?"

Dylan Kirby, at thirty-five years old, was four years younger than Fenton. He was tall and lanky with curly wavy brown hair down to his shoulders, and was one of the best engineers he had ever worked with. He was one of the funniest too—never too serious—but he knew his stuff. The man was a genius.

"Yeah, hopefully those photos will be from the Geneva of 2011," replied Fenton.

There was nothing he and Dylan could do at the moment. All the technicians and engineers were carrying out their final checks and only when they were finished could they begin their work.

"Dyl, do you fancy a coffee while we're waiting?"

"Sure thing, as long as you're paying," replied Dylan.

"Well since it's all free anyway," said Fenton, with a grin. "I'll treat you to breakfast as well."

"You're trying to spoil me again, prof," laughed Dylan.

* * *

Harry Stevens, the Defence Secretary was just leaving the Ministry of Defence at Whitehall and getting into his chauffeured car when Devon Miles, chief aid to the Prime Minister, approached.

"Mr. Stevens, may I have a word with you?"

"Certainly, what can I do for you, Miss Miles?"

"The PM has asked me to accompany you to PASTec. He wants an immediate first-hand report of the experiment. He would go himself but as you know the American President is here and he can't get away without raising suspicion."

"Yes, of course, please get in," replied Harry.

They drove most of the way in silence. Harry looked across at Devon, studying her as she rapidly typed on her notebook. At twenty-seven years old, she was superbly professional and amazingly intelligent. She sat relaxed and cross-legged. She dressed in a fitted pale blue suit that on most women would make them look masculine, but on Devon it just made her look all the more feminine. Combined with her natural straight blond hair that came to rest just at the top of her shoulders, her fair complexion, her blue eyes and her ready smile, she was stunning. Harry couldn't help but think how lucky the Prime Minister was to have an assistant as smart and attractive as her and with her political know-how, quick thinking, and astute observations. He also knew she had helped get the Prime Minister out of a few awkward and sticky situations professionally on many occasions. She was an asset he would have liked to have in his department instead of his current personal assistant, a Miss Aldridge, who was very good at her job. Justifiably, as she had done it for the past forty-four years, but she was not much in terms of eye candy.

During the journey, both became lost in their thoughts at the enormity of what they were about to witness if all went well and how it would change the world forever. They marvelled at how Britain was at the forefront of this mind-blowing technology, not counting the enormous financial benefits, but the possibility a man could be sent forward in time to bring back new defence capabilities, technologies that could make Britain the world's primary superpower once again. Advanced new medicines and cures to diseases could become available, never mind the fact that you could go back in time and influence the future to your country's benefit, avert or at least minimize past and future disasters, find new technologies in power generation—thereby eradicating fossil fuels. In addition, the DNA of long extinct animals could be brought back to repopulate. Just imagine woolly mammoths roaming free in the New Forest and the Scottish highlands. The list was endless. The potential benefit to mankind and to the world of sensible use of this technology was absolutely staggering.

The journey took almost two hours from Whitehall to PASTec and as Harry was not due at PASTec until eleven A.M., he decided to take a twenty minute break at the motorway services on the A3.

As they all walked into the coffee lounge, Harry looked across at George, his driver and protection officer. Not only was George an excellent driver with ex-forces pedigree, but he was also a personal friend. They had been friends when they were both in the Marines together, but Harry left and went into politics and George stayed on and joined the Special Boat Service. Harry was also George's and his wife Rita's son Steven's godparent. But despite this, Harry could not let on to his friend what he was about to witness. The PASTec program was above top secret. Many of the staff at PASTec did not even know what was being built there because it was purely on a need-to-know basis.

* * *

Terence Summerfield, the British Prime Minister sat in his office at Downing Street wishing he could be anywhere else today but here. He was also not sure if it was purely coincidental that the American President Leonard Cain had decided to make a trip here with just a week's notice, on the pretext that he wanted closer ties with his "favourite" European partner. He also had a suspicion that the PASTec program might have been infiltrated by the American intelligence services. Although the United States was no longer a superpower, since that position was now taken by China, they were still a major player in the world and could still wield significant influence, just as Great Britain still did well into the 21st century.

The Prime Minister walked into the main reception room and walked straight up to the American President and his wife, Roberta, and shook their hands. His wife, Kimberly, was already there making small chat about the President's children.

Leonard Cain was fifty-two, white, thin, tall at six foot two, and athletic-looking with short straight hair that was starting to show signs of gray. His wife was African American and in her early forties with what could be described as a full figure.

'Well, Terry, how are you? Your M.P.s' aren't giving you too much of a hard time, I hope?"

"No chance, I don't give them time to," replied the Prime Minister.

The Prime Minister was sure that just for a split second when he mentioned the word "time," he saw the President's eyes narrow. Leading them into the White Room he said, "Please sit, everyone. So, what really brings you across the pond at such short notice?"

"Well… Has there got to be a particular reason? I thought we could discuss current affairs that involve our two great nations, face to face. After all, it's not as if we don't have time," he said looking straight into the Prime Minister's eyes.

The Prime Minister stood up, noticing the emphasis the President placed on the word "time," and with an obstinate, fixed gaze replied, "Leonard, please follow me into my office next door. There is something I need to ask you before we have tea." The Prime Minister and the President stood facing one another, each equally as resolute. Each intently considered the other's gaze, trying to observe if he knew something.

"Well, Terry, what have you got to say that's so important that we cannot say in front of our wives?"

"You know damn well, Leonard: MI5 had an idea you had someone inside PASTec."

"Oh that old place where you've built a time machine," he

replied in an offhand way. "What made you think we had someone in there?"

"Very bloody funny!"

"Well, come on, Terry old boy, you don't think we could let you Brits have the monopoly on something of this magnitude, do you?"

"Why not?" replied the Prime Minister. "It was our home-grown scientists that designed and built it, with British taxpayers' money!"

"Yes, and thank you very much for that too," said the President—smiling smugly—knowing he still held the upper hand. "With our thirty-five trillion dollar debt, times are hard back home. It's easier for you Brits now that you're out of that E.U. club."

"So what do you really want Leonard?"

'Well, for a start, you could take me to PASTec today to watch the first test trial," he replied.

"Bloody hell, what the devil don't you know?" fumed the Prime Minister.

"What Professor Fenton had for breakfast," mocked the President.

"Christ!" the Prime Minister replied through gritted teeth.

* * *

Devon Miles was just being signed in at the PASTec reception by Stella when her cellular phone rang.

"Excuse me, Mr. Stevens; it's the Prime Minister on the phone."

Devon walked a few feet away from the reception desk and spoke into her cellular phone. Harry Stevens turned and looked just as Devon said, "What!?" to the Prime Minister and her face was drained white. "This can't be true, don't joke with me, Terence?"

"Who's joking," replied the Prime Minister, "I've never been more serious. The President knows all about the time machine program and he's insisting on being there today when we test it."

Harry Stevens walked up to Devon and asked, "Are you okay? You've gone pale."

"What... oh yes... no... I'm not all right. Bloody hell! No, sorry, sir, I was not talking to you, I was talking to the Defence Secretary. Can I call you back in two minutes?" Devon put the phone back in her jacket pocket and looked at the Defence Secretary. "The U.S. President is coming down to watch the test!"

"What!? What did you say?" replied Harry.

"Just that. Those bloody Yanks have had someone in here and know all about the project!"

* * *

Professor Fenton Jones and Dylan sat behind a row of computers checking and re-checking every piece of information the sensors were recording. The computing power needed to control, record, and analyze the time machine was enormous. Ten years ago, this would not have been possible due to the limited availability of computing power and speed, but now, due to the new types of quantum computers, this was possible.

The phone rang next to Fenton and he picked it up, "Hello, Professor Jones speaking."

Dylan heard a woman's voice at the other end but could not quite hear what she was saying except that the voice sounded very agitated. As Fenton shouted into the phone, Dylan realized that he had never heard the Professor ever lose his temper during the years he had known him. The man was always cool and calm and in control. The only time this veneer seemed to crack was when his wife left him a few years ago. "Who? What? Spy? When? The U.S. President coming here today? Delay the test? Orders of the PM?"

As the professor smashed the phone down, Dylan stood there staring at the professor just as did every single person in the Laboratory. Everyone was looking at Fenton. No one spoke and never had anyone seen the professor so angry that his face went bright red with rage. With that, Fenton stormed out of the laboratory.

* * *

Now the Prime Minister had another problem: how was he going to explain to the media that the President was going to a top secret British laboratory that was not on his official pre-planned agenda.

"Leonard, if you insist on going to PASTec, you do it my way: that means just you and two of your agents, along with me and my team of MI5 agents. No buts on this. It's my way or not at all. We will all get into the car in the underground garage and leave. The cars all have blacked out windows so no one should see us. So as far as the media is concerned, you are still at the Downing Street office. Agreed?"

"Agreed." replied Leonard, and a slight smile of satisfaction crossed his lips.

* * *

Harry Stevens and Devon Miles went through the laboratory's security procedures and entered the lab. Nothing could have prepared Devon for what greeted her eyes when they entered and looked up at the enormous machine directly in front of them.

"My God, just look at it. It's fantastic," said Devon to no one in particular.

Fenton recognized Harry, who had entered and strode across the lab so fast he was almost running. When he was about fifteen feet from the pair, he said to Harry, "What the bloody hell is going on? Have you heard about the Americans knowing all about this project and now it seems the U.S. President wants to watch? What does he think this is a Tuesday afternoon matinee at the Odeon?"

Harry offered out his hand to the Professor who just ignored it and continued demanding to know what the hell was going on. "Fenton… Fenton, please, calm down, lets go to the café, I'm in need of some caffeine and we can talk privately."

"After Devon received the call from the Prime Minister, I contacted the P.M as well and, yes, the Yanks have someone here. I have been in direct contact with the Security Services and they are sending down a team as we speak to see if they can find out who it is. Although as the cat is out of the bag now, so to speak, I'll expect the mole will probably reveal itself anyway, but what is done is done. What I am more concerned with is what do the Americans intend to do, it appears they want in, but only now that we have done all the hard work in designing and building it."

"Well, it's got to work first. It may not happen," replied Fenton,

"If anyone else had said that to me I might have had some doubt, but it's you I'm talking to. In the six years I have been Defence Secretary and was briefed on the time machine project I have never met a more determined, focused, and clever individual than yourself; to say you are a genius would be a vast understatement."

"Well, thank you for those kind words, Harry, but I'm still no wiser as to what the Yanks want."

* * *

The cavalcade, of two electric Land Rover Discovery 6's and a Range Rover Evoque Series 3, sped along the motorway at eighty-five miles an hour with the Prime Minister and the U.S. President in the bulletproof Evoque with the two CIA and six MI5 agents in the two Discovery's—one in front, and the other at the rear.

"Well, Leonard, if this experiment works and time travel becomes possible, where does America fit in this all-British Project?"

Turning in his seat to face the Prime Minister, the President said, "Look Terence, I'm going to be quite frank with you: we want the plans so we can build our own machine for ourselves. We won't take no for an answer. You can run your machine, but only under our control. Strict limits will be placed on how far forward or back you can go, and always under U.S. control. You will not be the world's superpower again. We will. If we have no control over your time travelling then you could go further into the future than us and pick up more advanced technology. Then we would have to go even further and it would end up as a time travelling arms race, and we cannot allow that."

With his anger surging up, the Prime Minister said, "And what if I say no, Leonard, what then?"

The President looked straight at the PM with eyes that suddenly became as hard as titanium and said, "Then my friend, there will be no time machine for either of us."

There was something in the President's gaze that made him feel true fear for the first time since he nearly drowned in a river as a teenager when his kayak overturned and was swept along into the rapids. He was only saved by the quick thinking of his sports teacher. Slowly and carefully, while looking straight at the President and emphasizing each syllable, the Prime Minister said, "What do you mean precisely by that, Leonard?"

"It means Terry, that if you do not do as told, the United States would be forced to launch a nuclear strike on mainland Britain ensuring the complete destruction of the PASTec Project and in doing so wiping out the whole of southern England including the city of London, thus ensuring almost every person involved in the project would be dead. With London gone and over twenty-five million dead, your little island nation will go back to the dark ages. So as I said, you will do as I've asked."

The British Prime Minister sat looking at the President with astonishment. He just could not believe what he had just heard his so-called friend saying, and for the first time he could ever remember, he was utterly speechless.

* * *

The three-car cavalcade pulled up at the main security gate and was waved straight through. Driving right up to the main reception entrance, the six MI5 and two CIA agents got out of the two Discoveries first. Looking around for anything that might be a danger, they then opened the two rear doors to the Evoque. Both the Prime Minister and the President got out simultaneously and walked straight into the reception, neither looking at each other.

Harry Stevens was standing just inside and held his hand out to the Prime Minister who ignored it. "This is the second time my handshake had been ignored his morning. I wonder if they're trying to tell me something," mused Harry.

Harry could tell something serious was up by the face on the Prime Minister. "Harry, we need to talk privately right now," the Prime Minister said through clenched teeth to his Defence Secretary.

"Certainly, sir, Stella, is there somewhere we can talk privately?"

"Yes, of course, please follow me. There is a room just around the corner."

As the door was closing, the Prime Minister exploded in rage, "Harry, they want the project, the whole bloody project. They'll let us use our machine but only on their say-so and under their direct guidance."

"What? Well, tell them to piss off. Who do they think they are?"

"Harry, if we don't do as they demand they'll nuke us. They'll wipe out the whole fucking south of England, including the capital!"

"You can't be serious. He's having you on."

"Harry, I'm deadly fucking serious. I assure you he means it," screamed the Prime Minister.

* * *

Devon Miles, along with two MI5 agents, led the U.S. President along with his two CIA agents to the security section of the time machine lab.

Devon had been appraised of what transpired between the Prime Minister and the President by Harry when he had come out of the

meeting. Harry had told her to take Leonard into the lab and intro-
duce him to the professor. Devon, like Harry and the Prime Minister, was seething, the sheer audacity and affront of threats to a
friendly nation and their closest ally was almost beyond belief.

"Okay, sir, please place your head into the retinal scanner, your
retinas will then be recorded for our records."

"What? I'm the President of United States, why do I have to go
through these procedures?"

"Because that *is* the procedure, sir, but of course, if you don't like
it we can always go back to the coffee lounge by reception."

The President was fuming at being treated like any normal
employee and it gave Devon enormous pleasure to watch. "Oh, by
the way, sir, your two agents will have to wait here."

For a moment she thought he was going to protest again, but he
just muttered something unintelligible. "Okay, Mr. President, now
if you would like to stand in that glass pod in front of you, Linda,
the security officer here, will scan you using the full body scanner."

This was almost too much for the U.S. President, as the scanner
saw right through all clothing, and the person monitoring the
screen would see everything, "*I will not!*" replied Leonard.

Very calmly and with a sweet little smile Devon replied, "Yes,
you will, or else it's the coffee shop. Procedures, remember?"

The President stood totally motionless, fuming as the scanner
scanned him from top to bottom. Just for the sheer hell of it, she
told Linda to scan him again, just to draw out his embarrassment
that little bit longer. The other side of the pod opened and Leonard
stepped through into the lab, immediately followed by Devon.
Leonard turned and said, "How come you did not get scanned?"

Smiling wryly, Devon said softly, "I don't intend to steal any-thing!"

She then lowered her eyes momentarily to his trousers and said, "Little man?"

Leonard turned and looked up. He was astounded at the enor-mous machine, so his rage and embarrassment of the previous min-utes faded away. Even though over the years he had had constant updates and reports on the project from his informant, nothing could have had prepared him for the sight of this vast machine. He stood transfixed, for what seemed like minutes, but was in fact only seconds. Devon was amused at the almost child-like look on the President's face as he stood in awe.

Professor Jones had seen Leonard Cain walk out of the pod into the laboratory with Devon Miles. All he knew was that security had been breached and the President now wanted to watch. He was totally unaware of the threat to the project and to the country at large by this man.

Fenton approached and said, "So, Mr. Cain, I hear you had somebody inside PASTec. You mind telling me who, so I can sack them?"

The President replied arrogantly and held out his hand, "Good morning, Professor Jones… Pleased to meet you too. I've had some good reports about you over the years!"

Fenton took an instant dislike to him but thought he had better not be outright rude. After all, he was the President of the United States. So with his right hand he made a play of scratching his arse, and then with it went to shake the President's hand. That will teach the bastard to send a spy in here, mused Fenton.

* * *

General Sir Stirling Davenport, Chief of the Defence staff sat in his Whitehall office talking to the Prime Minister and Harry via videoconferencing.

"Right, so let me get this straight, Prime Minister: you are telling me that the Americans know all about the time machine project. They had and still have a spy at PASTec, and are telling, not asking, for all the plans to said project, insisting on our subservience as to how and when we use it and if we don't comply with their demands they will attack us with a nuclear strike to wipe out the project and all who worked there. This result would effectively wipe out the whole of southern England, including London, killing tens of millions of people?"

"Yep! That's right. That just about sums it up," replied Harry.

"Christ almighty! They don't think that they can get away with that, do they? They are either desperate or mad."

"Thirty-five trillion dollars desperate, I'd say. Their country is broke, you know it, I know it, and the whole world knows it. The problem is they won't admit it. They see the PASTec project as a way out. The riches to be gained from this project are incalculable." replied the Prime Minister.

"Think about it," said Harry, "If they get control, they will reign supreme forever. Even if we attack them and hurt them, all they would have to do is go back in time and change the past to stop it happening. Think about it, Pearl Harbour, go back in time and warn the Pacific fleet of the day of the planned Japanese attack. They could give all details of the raid and the Pacific fleet would be intact and the Japanese fleet sunk. They could undo 9/11, go back, and kill Osama Bin Laden before he becomes a terrorist, resulting in over three-thousand lives saved. They could pass new laws to avert the banking crisis of 2009. The San Francisco Earthquake of 2017 could have deaths limited by evacuating the city before it happens. Never mind the catastrophic Asian floods of 2020. The list goes on and on."

"Then we have just two choices, as I see it," said Stirling. We either stop them attacking us by attacking them first, or we just hand over the plans and walk home with our tails between our legs."

"General, I want you to draw up battle plans with all the three Service Chiefs of Staff. I want a plan in front of me by 9 A.M. tomorrow morning. I want to know what realistically can be done, if anything."

* * *

The President asked, "Well, Professor, in layman's terms, how does this thing work?"

"Right, in layman's terms," replied Fenton. "Well, when the CERN Institute in Geneva discovered faster than light FTL Neutrino particles, known as tachyons, in 2011 using the Large Hadron Collider particle accelerator, it opened up the possibility of time travel. It has taken us almost eleven years to find out how these particles can be manipulated to fold subspace locally around it to create what is commonly known as a wormhole. A wormhole is basically a shortcut through space-time—from one place or time in the universe to another—by controlling the rate of energy and momentum. In doing this, one can transmit matter through this funnel in a controlled way. Then, the matter sent through would radiate negative energy particles for a limited period of time enabling the control centre here to keep a track on it and return it back to our space-time.

"Okay," said the President slowly, trying to take in what the professor had just said, "Surely it would take an enormous amount of energy to generate this subspace field?"

"Yes, you're right," replied Fenton, "that's why we have our own two nuclear reactors, PASTec A and B, each capable of 1150 megawatts. To run this machine we will need both reactors running at maximum output of 2300 megawatts. We also have the ability, if needed, to pull in more power from Hinkley point B power station in Somerset, which will provide us with another 1100 megawatts to the time machine. This would give us a total 3400 megawatts that we believe will be more than sufficient."

"How long does the negative energy radiate from whatever you send through the wormhole before it starts to decay and you lose the signal?"

"We estimate approximately ten to twelve days."

"What happens if you lose the signal, how do you bring back the item or human?"

"You don't. If the signal fails for whatever reason then he or she would be lost in time forever," replied the professor.

"So, what you are saying is that any time traveller would be limited in time travelling by time itself."

"In effect, yes," replied Fenton.

The Prime Minister and Harry walked into the Lab and along

with Devon walked up to the President, who was walking around the machine smiling with his hands in his pockets, "Impressive, very impressive, Terence. The reports I had from our contact here did not do this justice. Our scientists back home are going to think that Christmas has all come at once when they get their hands on these plans."

"Yeah, don't bank on it, sunshine," mumbled Harry under his breath. The Prime Minister gave his Defence Secretary a disapproving look to say to shut up, and then said, "Well, Leonard, so you approve of our little project, do you?",

"Oh yes, sure do, Terry old son, sure do indeed."

* * *

The group decided to break for lunch. Leonard was eating heartily, as did Fenton. The Prime Minister, Harry, and Devon ate a little but had no real appetite knowing what the man sitting opposite intended to do if he got his way.

Harry asked, "Leonard, how about us working as one team to share the benefit to both countries?"

Fenton responded, "What…? What's this? Share what?"

He looked at the President and said, "You're only here as an observer, aren't you?"

The President smiled, and with a slight nod of his head while looking at the Prime Minister, said,

"He doesn't know, does he?"

Fenton replied, "Don't know… don't know what? What the bloody hell is going on here? Is someone going to tell me or what?"

* * *

Inside a small conference room with Harry, Fenton exploded for a second time in one day, "This is a joke isn't it? You're having a laugh, please tell me," implored the Professor. "Please tell me this is a sick ministerial joke?"

Looking at the Professor, realising that apart from the political ramifications of what had transpired, Fenton looked like he was losing a child. This had been his brainchild for more than a decade and the product of working seven days a week, fifty-two weeks a year. He'd even sacrificed his private life when his wife Claire left him five years ago due to his near obsession with the project.

"I'm sorry, Fenton, truly I am, but we are not taking this lying down. As we speak the Joint Chiefs of Staff are meeting to find out what we can do militarily."

"Well, bollocks, I'm not going to do a test run with that…that *man* in my lab!"

"I understand your feelings, truly I do, Fenton. To say I could quite easily punch him into next week is an understatement, but the PM wants it to go ahead."

"Stuff what he wants, he's not getting it."

* * *

Eight MI5 agents entered the laboratory, including the head of the Security Services, Josephine Cameron, which just signified how serious things had become. Walking up to the Prime Minister, she said, "I hear we have a rat in the lab? We are checking every technician's personal details right down to the colored ink they use in their pens. Every computer, quantum drives, all deleted files, e-mails, cellular phone calls, and texts. Every home is being searched for anything that will give a clue, including bank accounts. I have over seventy operatives in the field looking into this along with the full resources of Thames House, along with MI6. Trust me, sir, if there is a spy in here, we'll get them."

* * *

Craig Stanton sat in the lab's CCTV control room watching the President closely on the monitor. He had been working for MI5 for just over twelve years and loved it. He knew what he was doing to help protect these shores from anyone who sought to harm Britain, whether it was her interests or her people. He had, like all the other agents, been informed what the Americans intended to do. Although he was incensed by their threats, he was not surprised. He had worked on joint operations a few times with the Yanks. That was before he found them to be, on a personal and professional level, arrogant bullies. This had gotten worse over the years the more it became apparent that they were no longer the superpower they once were.

His job was to watch Leonard Cain's every move. Hopefully he would give the game away with his operative by making contact with him or her. This strategy looked like it had worked, when two MI5 agents went up to the President and asked him to follow them; Craig noticed that he twice looked at the same technician standing at the foot of the gantry. The technician responded with a slight nod back. Using his cellular phone he called Josephine Cameron, "Ms. C., this is Craig in CCTV ops. The suspect is believed to be a male technician with short blond hair, glasses, dark trousers, and a brown t-shirt. He is standing at the base of the time machine gantry."

"Understood. Craig, good work. Stand by."

Josephine instructed three agents to detain the technician and to take him to a locked room outside the lab.

* * *

Josephine relayed the suspect's information to the Prime Minister. "His name is Lewis Rosen, thirty-three years old, British-born, but grew up in the States. After studying quantum mechanics and applied sciences at Princeton, he moved back here at the age of twenty-four. Both parents are professionals: his father is a lecturer at Oxford and his mother is a lawyer. Lewis has no criminal record, in fact, not even a parking ticket. We suspect the CIA recruited him while he was attending the university. He was considered by friends and colleagues to be outstanding in his field, which is why he was recruited for the PASTec program. He's a genius and cleared all checks by Security Services. He's admitted his involvement in the spying, but refuses to say why he did it!"

The Prime Minister was in no mood for niceties. "Get him off this complex and interrogate him fully. By the time you've finished, I want to know absolutely everything about him including how many times he shakes his dick after a pee."

* * *

The Prime Minister said, "Fenton… please listen. I know how you feel, but we still need to know if the time machine works. Too much has happened today, so I want the test postponed until tomorrow."

Reluctantly the professor nodded, "All right, but if it does work, I want first go at sending the President back to the Stone Age to see if he likes it."

* * *

Part of the PASTec installation had accommodation for overnight stays. Given this, Devon, Fenton, Josephine, and the President along with the dozen or so Security Service agents (including the two CIA agents) stayed at the complex; while the Prime Minister and Harry went back to London.

By the time they returned to Number 10, it was about seven P.M. On the way back, the Prime Minister had called for a meeting with all his senior ministers for an emergency meeting of COBRA. He went straight to the Cabinet room with Harry and met the rest of his Ministers and all the Chiefs of Defence.

"Evening everyone. I believe General Davenport here has briefed you all on today's events," said the Prime Minister brusquely, and everyone murmured in acknowledgment.

"I am not exaggerating when I say that the crisis that has developed today is probably one as critical as we have ever faced in our thousand-year history. So, in a nutshell, if we don't hand over all plans and rights to the PASTec program to the Americans, we will effectively be at war with the United States of America."

The Prime Minister let the facts sink in for a few moments before continuing. "We cannot go to the United Nations with this either because no one else other than those in this room, lab technicians, Security Services, and a few individuals in the U.S. administration know about it. Well, I hope only a few. If the whole world found out about the project, most of the world's leading countries would want it. With every major country wanting it for its own, chaos would reign. So what options do we have, if any? Would anyone like to start?"

General Sir Stirling Davenport, Joint Chief of the Defence staff, slowly rose and stood looking at all the men and women in the room before delivering his report. He then looked straight at the Prime Minister and said, "I have completed that report you wanted by tomorrow already, sir. Militarily, we have nine Astute-class attack submarines—each carrying sixteen conventional torpedoes—and four Poseidon class SSBN Ballistic submarines with sixteen missiles apiece. Each missile holds a ten-kiloton yield of twelve nuclear warheads, totalling 768 nuclear warheads, enough to effectively wipe out the United States. In summary, we have the capability to totally destroy the United States of America. The American forces have thirty-six attack submarines with twenty conventional torpedoes in each and fourteen SSBN ballistic missile submarines, each with eighteen missiles with sixteen ten-kiloton warheads. This totals 4,232 warheads; that's enough to effectively wipe out the planet, let alone little old blighty! If, for the sake of argument, we happen to know where every single American SSBN sub was at one moment in time—which we don't—and used all nine of our Astute-class attack subs and was lucky enough to sink them. Since they have fourteen, they could still strike Britain with the remaining five SSBN subs using the remaining 1,440 warheads. Never mind the fact that they have thirty-six attack subs out there hunting our nine

Astute-class attack subs. In other words, it's oblivion or total oblivion—a no-win scenario—the question is, are the Yanks bluffing? Would they really do it? If they did, then the only country that could stand up against them would be the Chinese, as they now see themselves as the world's policemen, but that would still be no good to us since we're all dead. We could protect our SSBN subs to some extent from the air, but that means carrier protection. We have two super carriers, the Queen Elizabeth and the Prince of Wales, and one aging helicopter carrier, the Ocean. Comparatively, they have eight super carriers; each of their carriers has more firepower than ours, so basically we're well outmatched. Our carriers would not have subsurface protection because our subs would be hunting theirs, but the Yanks have attack subs to spare, so good-bye three British carriers. At this point, we don't have any attack subs left to sink their carriers so they would still have eight; and then, of course, they still have all their land-based intercontinental ballistic missiles!"

"Thank you General, you've just made my day," replied the Prime Minister. "Has anyone else got anything to add?"

Carol Carter, the Home Secretary, stood. "It seems to me that the only advantage we have over them is the time machine program. If it works then, surely, that's the key. We can use it against them now, as the spy has been found and removed. The Americans will not know what we are doing as long as we do it soon, over the next few days."

"Well, that's okay, but we've still got the President to worry about," replied the Prime Minister.

"Why? He's a guest over here for the week. We still have six days before he is due back."

Harry said, "Are you saying what I think you're saying… to kidnap the American President?"

"Who said anything about kidnap," replied Carol, with an expression of faked innocence. "We're just putting him up for a few days at His Majesty's Pleasure."

"They'll go mad. They will demand to speak to him," replied Harry.

"Well yes," said Carol, "they'll huff and puff, start demanding this and that. We'll just say he's busy with matters of state with the Prime Minister. By then if the T.M. project works it won't matter. If it doesn't work by then, well, it won't matter either, as there will be nothing to fight over."

A smile started to spread across the Prime Minister's face and everyone started to laugh at the sheer audacity of it. "This just might work out after all."

CHAPTER 2

Tuesday, 9:17 A.M., Day 2

Leonard Cain lay back on his bed looking up at the tiled ceiling grid to his room. Outside stood two armed British Security agents. So much had happened in the last twenty-four hours or so that his mind was spinning. He needed advice from his advisors but the Brits had refused him any contact with his entourage of advisors, agents, and secretaries. The Brits had also removed the sub dermal locator in his left arm so that the Pentagon was unable to trace him. He stood up and went to the door to his room. He shouted through the gray locked door to the agents standing on the other side. "Don't you realize who I am? You can't keep me here against my wishes. You'll only make things worse for yourselves."

Getting no reply, he kicked the bottom of the door with his right shoe. "Shit, what do I do now?" he muttered to himself.

Leonard was used to giving orders and being obeyed. He was also used to having people around him to help him make the decisions needed. Now on his own he realized how much he relied on them for his decision making.

Craig Stanton stood outside the President's room with another colleague and smiled to himself. How could it get any worse, he

37

thought, they're threatening to nuke us, so stuff 'em if they do, then they'll cook their President too.

* * *

Carol Carter, the British Home Secretary was receiving calls from Leonard Cain's senior aid and also the American head of security who had been assigned to him over here for his week-long trip. They wanted to know where the devil he was. She realized she would not be able to ignore them for the few days they needed, so plan B was needed and quickly. The trouble was that she had no idea as to what plan B was.

Harry walked into the Cabinet office and saw Carol looking troubled and sitting there alone working on her handheld computer. He went up to her and said, "Bad night?"

"Bad night… bad night."

That's not the half of it, I've had the Yanks call me so many times insisting they speak to the President. I've kept telling them he is looking over a top secret installation and is busy; but it's just not washing with them. They know we've removed his sub dermal locator and they're going ballistic. They want to speak to him and now!"

Harry stood looking down at the Home Secretary and suddenly had a Eureka moment. Carol looked at him, "What's with you, you got fleas or something?"

"I think I've got it. I think I've got a way to give us the time we need."

* * *

The phone rang beside John Stewart's bed. He rolled over and looked at it. He thought about not answering, as he didn't recognize the number. Last night was a late night. Doing a two-hour stint on stage in front of a full theatre was mentally tiring, but he thought it might be important. He leaned over and picked up the call. "Hello?"

"Hello, is that Mr. Stewart? John Stewart?"

"Yes this is he. Who's this?"

"This is Harry Stevens, the Defence Secretary. We need your help. In fact, your country needs your help and we need it right now."

* * *

John was hurrying to get ready. He was told a car was on its way and would be there in fifteen minutes. He did not know what this was all about. He wasn't even sure if someone was having a laugh with him either, but something in the Secretary's voice told him this was real. He also recognised the voice as the Defence Secretary. He was an impressionist, so voices were his specialty. He quickly showered, dressed, and grabbed a quick coffee. Before he was fully dressed the doorbell rang. He answered the front door and saw two men standing there, one of them introduced himself as an MI5 agent and showed him his official identification. Realising this really was no joke, John let the one holding the badge enter. "Come on in, I'll be just two minutes."

* * *

As the car sped along the motorway, John was beginning to think now that there was something really serious going on as the car had four outriders with it. There were two police motorcycles up front and another two behind. The agents said they would be at Number 10 within forty minutes.

The car and outriders pulled up at the rear of Downing Street and went through the security gates. They drove straight down into the underground car park and stopped right by the elevator. He got out and entered the elevator with the two agents. The elevator took only a few seconds when the doors opened and the Prime Minister Terence Summerville greeted him himself.

The Prime Minister shook his hand firmly as he led him down a short corridor. "Good morning, John. Please come this way."

The two agents returned the way they had come. The Prime Minister was just as he looked on the television. He was short; about five foot seven, and had a stocky build with short cropped gray hair. Although he was fifty-five years old, he only looked in his mid to late forties. The Prime Minister walked into a long room with a large desk about thirty feet long and about eight foot wide at the end of which was a massive screen split into six sections with video of a large laboratory. The screens also showed statistics and battle plans with pictures of submarines and carriers. Another showed what looked like the President of the United States sitting in a small room looking at the floor.

Sitting around the large desk was the Home Secretary, The Defence Secretary and the joint Chiefs of Defence staff; The Prime Minister turned to him and said. "Please come on in and sit down. Welcome to the COBRA room of Number 10. I wish it could have been under better circumstances, but the situation is critical and we need your help urgently."

John Stewart sat there and listened intently to what he was being told by the Joint Chief of Defence. To say he was absolutely shocked was a vast understatement. The Prime Minister had decided to give him all the information about the crisis, in order to convince him to help at this level of involvement. He would need to know all the facts in order to complete the deception convincingly. When General Sir Stirling Davenport had finished his briefing, John turned to look at the Prime Minister, who said, "John, what you have just been briefed on is top secret. It must never leave this room. Do you understand the enormity of the situation?"

John nodded. "Yes."

Stirling handed John a two-page form. "Please sign this, John," said the General.

"What is it?" replied John.

"It's the Official Secrets Act."

John signed and dated it without even reading it. He handed it back to the Chief of Defence and looking back at the Prime Minister said, "Right. Exactly what do you need me to do?"

* * *

The desk phone rang in room 104 of the Ritz Hotel in London. Kurt Spitzer picked it up with his left hand before the end of the first ring. "Hello, Spitzer here."

The voice at the other end was the President's, as far as Kurt knew. "Hello, Spitzer. How are you?"

Spitzer immediately stood up ramrod-straight from his desk. Saluting with his right hand he said, "Good morning, Mr. President, how are you? We have been trying to contact you for the past fifteen hours."

"Yes, I know. I've been very busy discussing a top-secret project with the Brits, but I'm fine. Don't worry." John had been briefed on the President's staff and their names, but the Prime Minister and his staff did not know who, if any, of his staff had been informed of the PASTec program.

"Where are you, sir? This is *most* irregular, sir. Mr. President?"

"Yes, I know, but the Brits have asked me not to reveal their secret location, but I'll be back at Number 10 in a day or so. If you need to contact me at any time, call me back on this cellular number. Roberta is remaining at Number 10. I've already phoned her to let her know what I'm doing, so stop worrying. Don't forget I've still got my two CIA agents with me keeping me safe."

"Okay, sir, but when I spoke to the Vice President last night he was very concerned for your safety. He said something about not trusting the Brits anymore?"

"Well, can you phone him for me and tell him everything is fine? Tell him the Brits are coming around to our way of thinking. He'll understand what I mean.

"Very well, Mr. President, but this is still mighty irregular."

"As I said, Kurt, I'm fine. Look, I've got to go; the British PM has just walked in. I must go. I will contact you soon."

With that, John hung up.

The Prime Minister, who had been listening on a connecting line with Harry, said, "Phew, that was close. Do you think we got away with it?"

John replied, "Of course we did. I'm a professional, aren't I?"

They all looked at one another and started laughing.

* * *

After the call from the man Roberta thought was her husband, she felt happier. She knew the reason they had come to Britain was not just to work closer with America's close European ally. Rather, it was something very important for both countries, but she did not know any more. Since Leonard would now be away for the next day or so, she decided to go on the prearranged schedule of school visits and public speeches. The reason given to the media as to why the President was not being seen publicly was due to his having a bout of the flu; and he would be laid up for a day or so.

* * *

George was driving a limousine filled with the Prime Minister, Harry Stevens, General Sir Stirling Davenport, and John Stewart. Again with the same four police outriders—front and back—heading for the PASTec Laboratory. This left holding the fort, so to speak, back at Whitehall to Carol Carter, the Home Secretary, the Deputy Prime Minister, James Andrews, and Bill Oughton, the Foreign Secretary. Before the Prime Minister had left for PASTec, he had been advised by all the three Chiefs of Defence to put Britain's military into a high state of readiness. This included cancelling all leave, fuelling, supplying, and fully arming every operational naval ship, all four SSBN subs, and all nine Astute-class attack submarines. It also meant that all forty-two RAF Squadrons, including all reserves, were to be fuelled and armed to battle readiness.

The Government Communications Headquarters was in a high state of alert. Every piece of intelligence that could be gleaned from its many listening stations around the world concerning Britain and the U.S was being reported back to the defence chiefs and the relevant government ministers. The Army, with all regular and territorial soldiers recalled, was ready for civil defence in case of a nuclear attack. No reason was given except to the senior commanders, and only then just the basic information was conveyed.

MI5 and MI6 were calling on all their agents and contacts around the world for any piece of information that might be of use to Britain. All commonwealth countries were asked for any information they might come by to report it back to the British government. Also MI6's two agents hidden inside Langley, the CIA headquarters, were contacted and told to keep London informed on any piece of information, no matter how small. The media was only told that military exercises were being carried out for a mock nuclear attack. Food was to be stockpiled in all nuclear bunkers. Also before he left, he needed to inform His Majesty, King Charles, what had transpired in the last twenty-four hours and arrange for the evacuation of the royal family from British shores—first to the Ascension Islands, then on to Australia—all in total secrecy.

Since John was now right in the thick of it, Terence decided he should come along; as his voice could be needed at any moment, as events were very fluid.

Harry said, "I've spoken to Professor Fenton Jones just before we left, he said that the time machine preliminary tests had been completed and were awaiting our arrival before they start the first time travel test!"

The Prime Minister replied, "Fine. Do you realize that today, if the test is successful, will be a defining moment in time? The history of mankind is in the making with Britain right at the head."

They all looked at one another. No one said anything. Then the intercom came on and George, in front and behind the bulletproof glass said, "Sir, we will be at PASTec within ten minutes."

* * *

Everyone who wasn't needed for the actual test was sitting in an adjoining observation room. The U.S. President was left in his locked room and his two CIA agents were in a nearby room, still guarded by MI5 agents. The Prime Minister considered letting him watch but then thought better of it. He would get more satisfaction knowing that Leonard would love to be here watching, which gave him even more pleasure knowing he would miss it. In the lab, all the technicians were at their posts.

"Okay, all stand by," said the professor. Then he instructed one of his technicians to turn on the digital video camera and place it into the time displacement area of the machine. Climbing back down the metal gantry, he returned to his computer console. The professor then called out for confirmation from the power control technicians. "Power section?"

"Power availability levels at maximum."

"Telemetry?"

"Telemetry signal confirmed," replied another technician.

"Spatial Navigation control?"

"Spatial Navigation locked and confirmed."

"Do we have a green light on all subsystems?"

Then, one after the other, technicians called out, "Green, all green."

"It's a go, prof. Green here."

"And here, too, sir. All green."

"Okay, everyone," said the professor, "Now engaging Tachyon field!"

The machine started to hum. "Tachyon field stable. Now starting to distort the space inside the time portal area. The subspace wormhole is now starting to form," informed Dylan.

The Prime Minister and everyone else in the observation lounge stood. It felt like the air around them had begun to tingle. Looking up at the point of the wormhole—the area where normal space met the spatial distortion—an event horizon had started to form.

The Prime Minister said to one of the technicians standing close by, "What is that area of distortion we're seeing?"

"What you are seeing there, sir is the event horizon of an artificial stable wormhole that's connecting two worlds and times simultaneously by folding subspace."

The Prime Minister looked at the technician and wished he hadn't asked.

The President was sitting in his prison when he could suddenly feel the air around him tingle. He stood up and also noticed the lights in his room dim slightly. He realized that they were testing the time machine for the first time and wished to God that he was there watching it. He went to the door and kicked it again, demanding that one of the agents go get the Prime Minister. He wanted to watch the experiment, he wanted out. Both agents just stood motionless, smiling at one another.

The professor called out. "Subspace field stable. Transmit spatial coordinates of the CERN through the event horizon."

"Yes, sir," said the spatial navigation technician, "Transmitting coordinates 46 degrees 14`3``N 6 degrees 3`19``E by time dilation of 5,781,600 seconds for a fifteen Earth-second duration."

Everyone watched on the view screen, which was recording the event from just outside of the event horizon. They saw the digital camera that was being sent back start to dematerialise, after 1.3 seconds it was gone.

Exactly fifteen seconds later the video camera capturing the experiment recorded the small digital camera re-materialising back in the spatial portal. Dylan said excitedly, "The unit has fully re-materialised, prof!"

"Good, shut down Tachyon field now."

Instantly, the event horizon disappeared and the machine went silent, bringing to an end the tingling sensation, too. "Dylan, get up there and retrieve the camera."

"Sure thing, prof."

Dylan ran up the gantry two rungs at a time. He leaned into the time portal area and picked up the camera. Turning, he came down three rungs at a time.

"Okay, okay, give it to me, Dyl. I'll tie in the memory card to the main lab view screen and see what we've got," said the professor.

You could hear a penny drop as the professor linked the memory chip in. Everyone was looking straight at the view screen, and then there it was. First, it was recording the inside of the time portal. The visuals showed a haze for 1.3 seconds, and then a perfectly recorded CERN laboratory from 2011 appeared for 13.7 seconds. Haze appeared once again, but was followed this time by the inside of the time portal where it had re-materialised. An enormous cheer went up around the lab.

Dylan got under his desk and suddenly stood up holding two bottles of cheap champagne and two dozen or so plastic beakers. Popping the corks, he started to hand out the bubbly to everyone. The Prime Minister, Harry, the General, John, Devon, Josephine, and all the other technicians poured out of the observation lounge to congratulate the PASTec team and have a mouthful of the wet stuff. When the celebration subsided a bit, Dylan watched the recording again. He could not quite put his finger on it but something was nagging him in the back of his mind. It wasn't till the fourth time that it clicked. "Professor, quick, come here and look at this."

Suddenly it went quiet in the lab.

"What is it, Dyl? What you got there?"

Dylan replayed the recording back again and froze the picture after five seconds into it. "Look, prof!"

"Look at what?"

"You. There's you in the frame, standing behind that control panel."

"What? But that's impossible. I've never been there."

"Well, it appears you do go back in some future time. I suppose," he said, raising his left eyebrow, "nothing is impossible if you have your own time machine."

* * *

Richard Novak, the U.S. Vice President, sat in the Oval Office of the White House. He had just put the phone down from speaking to the President's senior aid, Kurt Spitzer, in London when he heard a rustle and something caught his eye. "Christ almighty, with all that's happening now we've got rats in the Oval Office!"

He called in an aid and told her to get the Rat Man in to get rid of the rodent, which she did and exited very quickly. Something did not feel right about the President going missing for fifteen hours. He knew the real reason why Leonard had gone to Britain. He also knew the Brits would not be at all happy at being forced to hand over the PASTec program and have their little island nation threatened with a nuclear strike. But this was a matter of survival. America was broke—bankrupt really—and they would never be able to repay the national debt which had reached an excess of thirty-five trillion dollars. With the time machine under U.S. control, there would be nothing they couldn't do. There would be total control of world events. There would be manipulation of foreign economies and of past events to enhance events of today to the benefit of the U.S. technologies of the future ensuring total military and technological supremacy. U.S. companies would be making cures for all diseases and selling them at massive profits. There would be new technology in power generation. Countries could be kept from getting too big and powerful—no one could ever threaten them again. If anyone tried, then the time travellers would respond with either total annihilation of the enemy or go back in time and stop the conflict before it started. He who controls the timeline controls eternity, for eternity. The U.S. could have absolute power over the world and beyond for all time.

The feelings of another sovereign state, even one as friendly as the United Kingdom, is irrelevant and inconsequential to the limitless power and wealth that would come from the PASTec program.

The U.S. was not prepared to share these vast and limitless benefits. America was totally committed to stealing the machine from Britain. no matter what the consequences or costs were.

* * *

The Prime Minister stood just inside the room where they were keeping Leonard Cain. Looking at the President, he glumly said, "It looks like we can all go home."

Leonard stood up quickly and said, "Go home? What you mean go home?"

"Just that, Leonard. It didn't work. We were unable to stabilize the wormhole, the event horizon began to expand and draw in matter from our time and space. We had to do an emergency shutdown; otherwise it would have drawn in the lab and everyone in it. Fenton said we were lucky and that it could have gone into a runaway cascade effect."

The Prime Minister had spent the last thirty minutes practicing that line.

"I don't believe you, Terence. Where is the proof?"

"Well, the Professor can explain it better that me, he understands all that technical jargon stuff. I'll get someone to go and get him, but considering the events of the last day or so, with what you and your countrymen intended to do, I can't say I'm sorry. You do realize relations will never be the same again between our two countries!"

The look on the President's face told the Prime Minister his ruse might just be starting to work. The professor had written a full report on the failed time travel experiment, ensuring it was full of technical language to make it appear believable to the American scientists. He could tell that the more he told the President what had happened using as much tech speak as possible, the more he appeared confused and unsure.

* * *

The Prime Minister along with Devon escorted Leonard off the PASTec complex into a waiting car along with his two CIA agents. They told the driver to take them straight back to the Ritz Hotel, where they would be leaving British soil on Air Force One at Heathrow by the end of the day.

A bullet proof blacked out Jaguar had been brought in, along with the same four police outriders, and sped away from the complex. Both Devon and the Prime Minister were visibly relieved on the walk back to the reception. "Well, do you think we got away with it, Terence?"

"Time will tell, Devon. Time will tell."

* * *

When the President arrived at the Ritz, he went straight to Kurt Spitzer and asked for an update on everything that had transpired while he had been away at His Majesties Pleasure. "Well, sir, the only major thing that had happened since I spoke to you on the phone earlier this morning was—"

"Hold on, hold on, Kurt. I spoke to you when?"

"This morning, Mr. President, at about 9:45."

"I don't think so, sonny. Those Brits never let me speak to anyone for the past twenty-four hours or so."

"Mr. President, I spoke to you on the phone. Look, I can show you. All calls are recorded as procedure. Here, listen."

Kurt went to his desk and played back the relevant recording and the President listened to himself speak to Kurt, just as he said. "Those slimy limey bastards, they've got someone to impersonate my voice. Why would they need to do that if the experiment was a failure? Something isn't right here."

"Er, experiment? What experiment is that, Mr. President?"

"What? Oh, never mind. By the way, what was it you were going to inform me of that had happened since that faked call?"

"Well, this is mighty strange, sir. A few hours ago the Brits put all, and I mean all, their defences into a state of battle readiness. It's as if they're about to go to all out war."

* * *

Richard Novak, the U.S Vice President, was sitting in the White House Oval Office with all his Joint Chiefs of Staff. When one of the phones rang on his desk, he picked it up and heard the President on the other end. "Richard, I'm on my way back early. I want to know what's been developing while I've been away."

The Vice President activated the speakerphone so that the rest of the room could hear. "Thank God, Mr President. We've been going frantic not being able to contact you. Are you all right, sir?"

"Yes, of course, I'm fine. The Brits wanted to show me some top secret project they had, but the experiment failed; so back to the drawing board for them and us."

"Mr. President, it's okay to talk, the only people who are in the room are the Joint Chiefs of Staff who already all know about

PASTec program."

"Oh, right, er, well can you give me an update on anything you think I need to know about?"

Richard looked at the others in the room and then looked at the phone. "Sir, are you all right?"

"Why, yes, of course, just a little, er, tired."

With that, another phone rang on the desk and looking at the Vice Chairman of the Joint Chiefs of Staff who nodded to say 'answer that call', picked up the phone and said, "Admiral Peter Cartwright."

"Hello Peter, it's Leonard, is Richard there?"

Admiral Cartwright just stared at the phone and then at Richard on the other phone, who was also speaking to someone identifying himself as the President.

"What the devil is going on here? We've got two Presidents on the phone." Immediately realising one was an impostor, he said. "Richard, take it off speaker and ask him the first line of his encryption code to take us to DEFCON 3!"

Richard asked the imposter and the phone went dead.

"Fucking hell, those Brits… the bloody audacity of it!"

On the other phone, the President was calling out about what the hell was going on. "Mr. President, you are not going to believe this, but…"

* * *

That's all really the Prime Minister wanted to know. Although it's a shame that they twigged it was an impostor, he got the information he needed. Now he knew that all the senior military people in the U.S. administration were in on the threat to the United Kingdom. Knowledge combined with a time machine was power.

* * *

Professor Fenton Jones sat with Dylan in the laboratory checking the data received during the time experiment. They checked and re-checked all the information stored on the quantum computers. "Prof, look at this here. This is the readout from the power generation section during the test."

"I see what you mean. They should not be fluctuating like that. The power levels used should have been a constant increase in energy going back in time until the camera reached a set point in space-time. Then a gradual decrease in energy would be visible as it returned to present time."

Dylan then said to Fenton. "Look as this too, prof. The containment field has fluctuations in its field density."

"That's not good either, Dyl. By the way, when the test was going on, did you feel a tingling sensation?"

"Yes, now that you mention it, I did. It felt like all the hairs on my body had suddenly stood on end. I thought it was just me with the excitement?"

"No, I felt it too."

He called over to Liz, one of the other technicians sitting on another console nearby. "Did you feel a tingling sensation too, during the test?"

"Yes, professor, I did, but I thought it was just me!"

* * *

Terence Summerfield, Devon, the General, Harry, and Josephine sat in the main conference room of the PASTec complex, along with the professor and Dylan. Everyone in there had been fully apprised of the situation and how critical events had become.

The Prime Minister said, "Professor, the need for speed is critical. We need to send a human through as soon as possible."

"What? You've got to be mad. We've only tested it once and that was on an inanimate object. We haven't tested it yet on living tissue!"

"Then you had better hurry up, time is of the utmost importance."

"But we're still examining all the test results. It could take weeks."

"Weeks? No, no, today—I want the test done this afternoon."

"Impossible, absolutely not. You're going too fast. I need to study these results more closely."

"And if you do it my way—and it works—you will have all the time in the world."

* * *

Air Force One was heading back to the United States, at almost seven hundred miles an hour, with the President and his wife. Leonard Cain was in constant contact with all his senior Defence Chiefs, Vice President, Director of the CIA, and his most senior senators and aids who were privy to the British time machine project. They all knew of the President's plan to steal the program.

"So, the Brits have put all their defences on red alert, even though supposedly the time machine does not work. What do you make of this, Admiral?"

"It's hard to say, Mr. President, they may have put all their defences on alert because of what they think we might or might not do. It's a sound military tactic. I would do the same if I was them, sir. However, if the time machine does work and we find out, then it would still make sense to put their defences into alert status. So, what I'm saying, Mr President, their military being on high alert does not confirm if the machine works or not."

"We need to definitely know if it works. We need someone in there again. Have we heard anything about Lewis Rosen? What have the Brits done with him?"

The Vice President looked up and said, "No, sir, we've heard nothing since MI5 detained him. We believe he is being questioned at Thames House. We have told them we want him back immediately, but the Head of MI5 Josephine Cameron told us—and I'll quote—'He's taken time out to help with their enquiries.'"

"Right, so we have to assume we have lost that asset. Where do we go from here?"

Admiral Cartwright replied, "Well, for a start, I think it would be wise to put our military on alert status, too. We don't want to be caught with our pants down, so to speak."

"Agreed. See to it immediately, Peter."

"Yes, sir, Mr. President."

* * *

In the laboratory, Fenton, Dylan, and other technicians were hurrying through their tasks. The Prime Minister had ended up ordering the professor and his team to go to the next phase of the test and send through a live animal. Fenton was not happy about this, he was having no time to check and analyze any of the results of the previous test.

Harry asked, "Well, professor, what are you going to send back and where in time?"

Dylan looked at the professor and smirked, "Well… we thought we would send back two fully grown rats."

The Prime Minister enquired, "Yes, but when and where in time?"

"Well, er, well… we thought… well, that is, the professor and me…"

"Yes? Well, out with it, come on, where and when?" asked Harry

"Er, five hours back in time."

The Prime Minister shouted, "Where?"

"The White House Oval Office. I thought the rats would feel at home there."

The whole laboratory erupted in laughter.

* * *

The rodents were placed just outside of the time displacement area in a cardboard box. There was a technician standing by to insert them in when instructed to.

"A technician said, "Subspace field stable." "Power generation at maximum," said another technician.

"Okay, insert Roland one and two into the time displacement area now."

"Enter spatial navigation coordinates of the White House Oval Office."

"38 degrees 53`51`` N 77 degrees 2`11``W by 18,000 Earth Seconds."

"Telemetry locked, receiving signal."

"Tachyon field engaged and locked."

The machine began to hum again and a wormhole formed. Everybody started to feel their skin begin to tingle again. Only this time, it was much stronger.

The rodents dematerialized after 1.3 seconds and were watched again on the view screen just outside of the event horizon.

After fifteen seconds, rematerilization was initialized, but when they all looked at the view screen only one rodent had reappeared. Fenton said, "Damn. We have a problem, only one returned."

"Er... no... no problem, professor, I, er, deliberately left one behind," said Dylan.

The professor shouted, "What? Why?"

"Well," Dylan grinned. "A little memento of the President's visit. I thought it might help out with American relations!"

* * *

The media were starting to catch on that something was up. They had heard from various sources that the British and American military had been mobilized. Additionally, they had not been fully convinced that this was just military exercises and were also suspicious since the U.S. President and his wife had gone home on the second day of a six-day visit. The couple had hardly been seen when they were abroad. Carol Carter, the Home Secretary, had been taking the full flack from the media and also from her own members of Parliament. Parliament wanted to know what was going on and where the Prime Minister and Defence Secretary were. Now that the Prime Minister and Devon had returned to Number 10, and left Harry

Stevens at the PASTec lab, hopefully they could calm some nerves. The Prime Minister, with Devon at his side, made a statement on Downing Street. He reiterated what the Home Secretary Carol Carter had said earlier and assured the media everything was fine. These were just joint Anglo American military exercises practicing for war against rogue nuclear states and would be lasting for a week.

* * *

Terence, with his wife Kimberly, sat opposite Devon and General Davenport in the White Drawing room reviewing the day's events and their options. This room was the Prime Minister's favourite room at Number 10. He was always able to relax more here when in meetings than in any of the others. Tomorrow, he intended to send a human through time. If all was successful, then a plan needed to be formulated to beat the Americans through time itself. Privately though, he began to wish the time machine had never been developed. Life would have been so much easier.

CHAPTER 3

The President needed to know what was going on inside PASTec. He needed to know if the test was a success or not. Either way, he wanted the plans and schematics from the program. If it worked, then fine. If it failed the Brits must still be close to success, so in American hands they should be able to finish off the project. But if the Brit's managed to get it working before an up and running U.S. version was completed, the British could manipulate time and stop them and they would never know. Sitting in the Oval Office of the White House Admiral Cartwright said, "Mr. President, the situation has now changed. It may be too late if you decide to nuke the U.K. due to the fact that the time machine could already be up and running. Given the situation and the urgency to get the plans before the British can manipulate time in their favour, I recommend a Special Forces infiltration of PASTec."

"And how do we do that?"

"We send in a Carrier Strike group of three Gerald R. Ford-class super carriers, three Zumwalt-class destroyers—which have all just been installed with Free-Electron Laser-directed energy weapons—

61

along with submarine cover of four Virginia-class attack subs which were complete with Tomahawk missiles. That carrier group alone is equivalent to about half the size and power of the Royal Navy. Then we send them off the coast close to Portsmouth, the city that is the home of the Royal Navy. Don't forget, sir, we are supposed to be all best buddies and we're having war games so they won't be able to say no. Then we send in Special Forces using four stealth Chinooks at night. We can easily get thirty-five soldiers in each with all necessary equipment. The Chinooks fly in low, and at maximum speed of two-hundred miles an hour we can get from the carrier group anchored just off in the Solent to the PASTec installation in about twenty minutes. Then we storm the installation. They won't be expecting an attack of that magnitude, we will overrun the installation killing anyone who tries to stop us, get all computer records and then kidnap the professor and his sidekick Dylan. At the same time, we plant explosives around the time machine and destroy it, thus giving us the time to build our own."

"But then the cat will be out of the bag. Wouldn't the world know what we have done?"

"No, not necessarily, Mr. President" said the Admiral.

"What do you mean?"

"Well, they have two nuclear reactors there. We destroy one. We don't destroy just the time machine—we destroy the whole complex. It then looks like a nuclear accident, and besides I can't see the Limeys admitting that we destroyed their complex openly. They will have to cover it up somehow!"

"How long will it take to get our assets into position, Peter?"

"That's the problem: at maximum speed across the Atlantic, it would take two and a half days. I've taken the liberty of ordering them to set sail for British waters already. They left Norfolk Naval base early this morning"

"Good work, Peter. Inform all heads of Departments of Defence. It's a go."

* * *

Harry stood there looking at the machine and then at Fenton, "No, Fenton. No, this test must be today—this morning, in fact. I don't care if you have weeks of analysis to do, we need to send a human through. We need to know what the Yanks are up to, and we need to know now."

"Yes, I understand the urgency. It's just that both times we acti-vated the machine we were getting unexpected readings."

"What unusual reading? I thought it all went fine?"

"Well, yes, the fact we sent things through time twice and were successful is not the issue. Look, this is what I'm talking about!"

Fenton showed Harry the report on the power fluctuations and the fluctuations in the density containment field. "This could be serious; the fluctuations were higher on the second time."

"What could happen if these fluctuations increased?"

"I wish I knew. It seems to me that something is drawing more power from the power plants than is needed and that increase in energy is causing the field density to destabilize to a degree. If it destabilizes too far, the wormhole could become uncontrollable and would start to draw in anything it can get."

"What do you mean by anything?"

"It could, in theory, swallow everything: you, me, the laboratory, the building, or even time itself. Like a black hole in space, the more mass it swallows, the bigger and more powerful it gets."

Fenton stood there letting this information sink in for the Defence Minister for a few seconds.

"Right, but if this happens, can't you just turn the power off? Surely that would shut it down."

"It might and it might not. This is all uncharted territory. The extra power it's drawing, it seems to be able to store it somewhere in subspace. It may be able to sustain itself, so shutting it down on this end might not work. That's why we need time to analyze the results."

"Look, I understand what you are saying but the situation is critical. I've just had the General on the phone; he's informed me that there is an American carrier group heading across the Atlantic. They'll be in our waters within sixty hours. That's how long we've got!"

* * *

Harry Stevens was taking a walk around the grounds of PASTec. He was trying to get some fresh air and clear his head. This was one of those defining moments in time—a pivotal point in history—and he tried to make sense of everything that had happened in the last forty-eight hours or so. No matter what happened, nothing would ever be the same again.

He thought about his wife, Joan, back home in London. He thought that he should call her and let her know he was fine. He also thought about the twins who had just gone to Oxford University and wondered how they were getting on. There was so much he should do. It was just finding the time. "I'll call her later, when it's quieter," he said to himself.

He now had to decide what member of the program to send through. He did not want a scientist, as he thought that with the known problems with the machine, their expertise should be this side of time where they could try to resolve it. Also, whoever went through would be put into a military situation, so he wanted a person with that type of training. He also needed to be able to trust that individual, and the only person he could think of at this short notice who met that criteria was his driver, his protection officer, and his best friend: George "Nobby" Clarke.

* * *

George sat in the observation room that adjoined the lab, listening to his friend Harry tell him all about the time machine program and what had transpired with the Americans. He sat there without saying a word from start to finish. When Harry finished explaining, he said to his friend, "I can't force you to go George. I'm asking you as a friend, your training as a Special Forces soldier makes you the ideal candidate. I won't lie to you, it's dangerous. You might get killed, or worse, you might be trapped back in time. But I need someone I can trust implicitly and that's you, my friend. Think of it like this: you will be the first human ever to travel in time; you'll be up there in the history books along with Neil Armstrong, Columbus, and the Wright Brothers. Your name will live on in history books forever.

* * *

"Right, George, it's a gamble that no one will be in the Oval Office at three A.M. We will insert you there, and you will have sixty seconds to plant the listening device. Then you will be returned here, checked, and then be immediately reinserted twenty-four hours later in their time to retrieve the device. We must know what their plans are."

"Don't worry, Harry, compared to some of the ops I've done in the SBS, this will be a piece of cake."

Just as he was about to climb up the gantry to get into the time displacement area, George turned to Harry and whispered into his ear. "If something does happen, Harry, promise me you will look after my family?"

Looking straight into George's eyes, he said, "I swear, Nobby, I swear!"

* * *

George lay there looking up at the ceiling of the machine. He could hear all the technicians talking to one another and heard the machine hum loudly. Then he felt a tingling feeling all over and everything blurred for a second or so. Suddenly, he found himself lying on the floor of the Oval Office.

He quickly stood, and feeling sick, he paused for a moment to let it pass before looking around the empty room. "Thank God," he murmured to himself.

God almighty this was incredible, it really does work, he thought. He walked across to one of the windows and looked out of the Truman balcony onto the south lawn to see the Washington Monument and fountain lit up at night. He saw the cars driving about, people walking past, and realized none of them had any idea what their government was intending to do. To think we were almost at war with this country, he thought.

He heard talking from somewhere outside in the corridor, but the sound was fading. He quickly placed the listening device under the ornate table near the window, and looked at his stopwatch and realized he only had eight seconds left. He quickly lay back down on the floor. He did not want to be re-materialised inside the machine itself. With that, he heard a slight hum. His vision blurred again for a second, and then he was back in the lab. He gave the thumbs up into the camera that was just outside the event horizon. Then his vision blurred again. He was again laying on the Oval office carpet and nausea swept over him. He quickly stood and removed the listening device, turned, and looked down at the resolute desk. With a grin, he sat in the President's chair and picked up one of the three pens that had "President Leonard Cain – White House" written down the side and placed it into his shirt pocket. Once again, he got up and lay back down on the floor. After a few moments, his vision blurred again and he was back at the lab. He went to crawl out but could not, as the machine was still running. The event horizon was still there. He could see through the event field and could see all the technicians working frantically at their consoles. Everyone had worried looks on their faces. Harry just stared up at him with a look of horror. After what seemed minutes, he heard a loud popping sound, what sounded like water rushing over his head, and then just silence. The event horizon was gone. He crawled out and quickly slid down the metal gantry, feeling the familiar nausea. "What the hell happened? God, I feel sick." said George.

The professor replied, "Bloody hell, that was close."

George looked at Harry. "What was the problem? It looked like you had problems shutting down?"

"They did. There is a problem with it and we're not giving the professor and his team enough time to sort it out," replied Harry. "Well, did you manage to do it?"

"Of course I did. By the way I've a present for you, courtesy of Leonard himself."

* * *

The Prime Minister, Devon, all the Chiefs of Defence, Deputy Prime Minister James Andrews, the Home Secretary, Carol Carter, and William Oughton, and the Foreign Secretary all sat round the large desk in the COBRA room at Number 10 talking to Harry Stevens via videophone link on one of the large plasma screens up on one end.

Harry had already listened to the recording of the President and Vice President's plans to send in Special Forces to wipe out the PASTec complex. Now he played it back again to them all at Number 10. "Well, they certainly mean to take it out, don't they? The only good news is that they don't seem so eager to nuke us now, since they think we have the time machine operating or at least nearly completed."

The Foreign Secretary said, "Then our next problem is going to be that carrier group on its way. What can we do to stop it getting into British waters?"

General Sterling Davenport looked up and said, "Militarily, we can stop it. We can sink the lot; but the political ramifications would be enormous. How would we explain to a shocked world that the Royal Navy sunk an entire American carrier strike group in international waters during what was supposedly military exercises?"

"Well, as I see it all we can do is let them anchor off in the Channel. We let their four Chinooks fly in and when they are over open countryside, shoot them down." said Bill Oughton. "They won't be expecting us to know and the Yanks won't be able to accuse us openly as they shouldn't be there in the first place. We'll just make a statement saying that there was a catastrophic accident involving British and American military maneuvers over the British mainland."

"Anyone else got any better ideas?" asked the Prime Minister, as he looked around at everyone in the room. No one spoke.

"So, it's decided then. We shoot them down," said the Prime Minister.

To which the Joint Chief of Staff responded, "Sort it, General. Take 'em down."

* * *

Fenton and Dylan, along with the other technicians, worked almost around the clock trying to work out what the problem was with the time machine. Until they could find and rectify it, Fenton was very reluctant to let anyone or anything go through the machine.

"So, what do we know about the fault?" asked the professor.

"Well, each time we use the time machine we get an increase in power usage, but it fluctuates wildly. I cannot figure out why, since the power is not being used for the time travel itself, however it seems to be being drawn to the wormhole and is causing the field density around it to begin to destabilize," replied Dyl.

Liz, another senior technician said, "If the field density becomes so unstable and collapses altogether, what would happen to the wormhole?"

"That's a total unknown, we are all in uncharted waters here," replied the professor.

"Speculate," said Dylan.

"Well, we can always shut the power off. It's not too bad. Although if there was anyone in the machine at that time we could lose them either in time itself, or they may not be rematerialized correctly. Their matter may be spread out over the timelines."

Liz said, "Prof, look at this readout. I've just noticed something strange!"

"What have you got there, Liz?"

"Right, look at this. We used at this point in the experiment 2050 megawatts of energy, of that 1670MW was being used for the time travel, which left 380 megawatts of energy going elsewhere. But look here, the wormhole was registering 570 megawatts. However, it should not be registering anything. It's a negative energy field. During the previous test with the rats, the wormhole registered 190 megawatts, the wormhole seems to be drawing excess energy and storing it up. So when we turn it on again the wormhole is already charged, that again draws more energy. It is this energy that I believe is destabilizing the field density"

"Fenton, I do think she's got something there," said Dylan.

"Then what you are saying is there could come a time when we won't be able to shut it down because of all the stored energy in the wormhole?"

"Exactly," replied Liz.

* * *

Harry Stevens was with all his Chiefs of Defence in Whitehall, London. He was discussing plans to shoot down the American Chinooks. "Just to be sure, there will be three lines of defence. Knowing their planned route makes this easier. They would for speed—and thinking we would not know of their raid—take the most direct route from their carriers in the Solent to PASTec, a distance of fifty three miles. One line of defence will be in the woods north of Petersfield spread out over a ten-mile radius. The second line of defence is in the woods between Bordon and Liss. The third, and last, line will again be in woods and just to the south of the PASTec installation, west of Aldershot. Weapons to be used will be the man-portable Starstreak Mark III surface-to-air missile. Radar will be tracking the choppers and when they are within range and over open countryside, the Army will take them out. Recovery helicopters and vehicles will be near all three locations to remove all debris before any civilians arrive on the scene. The first things to be removed must be the pilots, crew, and anything else that would show an observer it was American."

* * *

Back in the lab, the professor and his team were still working on the fault with the time machine.

"By my estimates, prof, within the next two to three time travel trips we could be looking at losing control of the wormhole due to the stored energy within. When that happens, we would no longer be able to shut the wormhole down from this end. We would have to wait until the energy stored within the wormhole gets used up," said Dylan.

"Any idea how long that would be?"

"How long is a bit of string?"

Liz suggested, "How about turning on the machine and then cutting the power to it? We wouldn't be sending anyone through and we could let it sit in neutral, so to speak, and see if we can find that energy drain to the wormhole that way. At the same time, we would let the wormhole drain its own stored energy away."

"Well, that's as good as any idea so far. We have about two days to sort it before that U.S. battle fleet turns up on our doorstep and the PM will want us to use her again."

* * *

The Prime Minister was sitting opposite Devon in the White Room at Number 10 Downing Street. A tray of tea and biscuits sat on the coffee table in front of them. The Prime Minister dunked his biscuit into the hot liquid and said, "Devon, so far we have been on the defensive. We react to the Americans' actions. We need to change this and get them to react to us. We need to take the initiative. After all, we have the advantage of the time machine. It's about time we used it to keep them on the back foot for a change."

"So, what do you propose, Terry?" asked Devon.

"I propose to use the machine to greatly damage their capability to harm us. I propose to send back a small team to 1961 to plant a small, but powerful, nuclear device under a military installation that is just starting to be built at that time. It will be activated by remote control from one of our orbiting satellites now in present time. That will prove to the Americans that we won't be pushed around and told what to do!"

Answering slowly and looking straight at the Prime Minister, she said, "Where are you going to plant this bomb?"

"Under the NORAD Cheyenne mountain range. I'm going to bring down the entire North American Air Space Defence Command Center."

* * *

Harry had been apprised of the Prime Minister's plan by Devon and had doubts about it. Part of him agreed with his plan, especially since the U.S. was prepared to nuke them, but another part of him felt it was a plan that could push them too far and make them act more rashly. Especially considering that the Canadians also used the facility, he felt they would be inadvertently attacking a very close and friendly Commonwealth nation. But if the Canadians were warned about the attack, it would surely compromise the operation. He also knew the Prime Minister was right, they were reacting to U.S. actions and soon they would make a mistake. The U.S. would have the upper hand and they would lose control, but it just felt wrong, though he could think of no other alternative. The Prime Minister instructed he wanted the bomb planted before the U.S. carrier group arrived in U.K. waters, but not detonated till after the shooting down of the Chinooks. The Prime Minister wanted it done like this for more impact on the Americans. He was also instructed that when the U.S. carrier strike group was in the channel off Portsmouth, to have a show of force from the Royal Navy. He wanted both Britain's super carriers in the Solent along with three Astute-class submarines and four Type-26 Frigates and two Type-45 Destroyers. If the Yanks got pissed off because the U.K. shot down their choppers and then find out they took out NORAD, they might get trigger happy. A show of force from the Royal Navy might just deter them from doing so.

Harry sat in the small garden at the back of his Whitehall office. The sun was shining warmly in a clear and almost cloud free sky. The wind was light and he could hear the sound of birds chirping in the trees and bushes around him. He was surprised at just how quiet the sound of the city was, seeing as he was sitting right in the center of Westminster.

He picked up his pocket mobile computer and dialed his wife. He hadn't spoken to her in the last three days and thought it best he call her as she had left eleven messages in his inbox along with eighteen missed calls. He found that he was smiling to himself thinking that he was not sure who he'd prefer to deal with, his wife or the Yanks.

* * *

Fenton looked across at Dylan and realized he was exhausted. They all were. He made a decision. "Right, that's it guys, we've been working nearly fourteen hours today, sixteen yesterday, and so that's it. Go home all of you."

Fenton looked at his friend and said, "That order includes you, mate. Home, now."

"I'll tell you what, prof, I'll sleep here. It's easier," replied Dylan.

"Oh no, you won't. Otherwise you'll be back here at your desk in a couple of hours. I'll tell you what, come back home with me, we'll get a bottle and some carry-out on the way home. It's better than eating on my own in an empty house."

"Okay, as long as it's Indian."

"It's a deal."

As they walked out of the lab, Dylan turned to the professor and asked, "What's their Bombay Potato like?"

* * *

"Do you ever regret the work we do at PASTec?" asked Dylan.

Both Fenton and Dylan sat in two big cottage wing chairs covered in green tapestry fabric with Queen Anne legs. They ate their curry and sipped glasses of cheap medium-dry white wine. Soft jazz music played quietly out of the C.D. player of an old fashioned stack system in the corner.

"Yes and no is the answer to that."

"In what way?"

"I love my job, to be part of this project, to be part of history, to be able to change history to man's benefit. I wouldn't have wanted to do anything else."

Dylan raised his left eyebrow. "But?"

"Yeah… but. But if it wasn't for this job, I would still be married to Claire."

"You still miss her?"

"Every bloody day!"

"Sorry, prof, didn't mean to pry."

"No…no, that's okay. Just gets a bit lonely and I start feeling sorry for myself sometimes."

"Don't we all? I've not had a bird in the past eighteen months."

"You frustrated git!" replied Fenton laughing.

CHAPTER 4

The sky was leaden gray and threatened rain at any minute. It cast the whole complex in a colourless hue, and made everything appear dull and drab. The green Army truck carrying the nuclear device pulled up at the PASTec main gate. Security had been informed of the arrival of the truck along with eight SAS Special Forces, four in the truck and another four in two separate Land Rover Discoveries—one in front and the other at the rear. The vehicles drove straight in and parked at the rear of the building next to a large blue loading bay door. The bomb's weight was just 370 pounds and was three feet seven inches by four feet ten inches long. It had an explosive yield equivalent of approximately five million tons of T.N.T. The bomb rested on a small metal frame with casters for maneuverability. The device had been installed with a very high frequency and powerful receiving device as the remote detonation signal would have to penetrate solid rock. The bomb was wheeled into the laboratory through the loading bay doors and block-and-tackled into position just outside of the time displacement area.

All of the coordinates had been inputted into the quantum

computers and four SAS soldiers were sitting inside the time displacement area. The group was ready for time slip back to 1961. Their instructions were to ensure that no one was about. They were to be inserted in time at 2 A.M. local time. Hopefully no building contractors would be about. If there were, then they were instructed to remove them permanently. The bomb would follow through time thirty seconds later (their time) followed by the remaining four Special Forces. They were to be given one hour to complete their mission and get ready for their extraction back to the present.

Fenton shouted, "No! No! You cannot do this. I told you yesterday the machine is not functioning properly. We estimate that the machine might become out of control due to the power build-up within the wormhole. We might lose your assets or worse."

"Sorry, it can't be helped. It's a chance we've got to take. The situation is critical and this order comes from the Prime Minister directly," replied Harry.

"But it's not a chance you are taking, it's a chance those guys are taking."

"Fenton, just do it. We don't have the time for this health and safety stuff. Just send them back in time!"

* * *

The taxi pulled up at the main gate of PASTec and moaning Martin the security guard was on duty. He looked in the back, saw an old man who he estimated to be at least ninety, and said, "Can I help you?"

The voice that replied was surprisingly deep and rich. "I hope so. I need to speak to Professor Jones or Harry Stevens urgently."

"Who are you?"

"A very old man who has one last job to do!"

"They are not here."

"Yes, they are. Just phone them and tell them I'm here. Here's my name." The man handed the guard a card with his name on it. "Go on, young man, hurry up. I don't have all day."

* * *

The four SAS lying side by side inside the time displacement area, heard a loud hum, felt a tingling, and then suffered blurred vision for a moment. They found themselves in an enormous cave with sporadic lighting around the walls that gave the cave an eerie glow. They immediately spread out and then heard a hum when the bomb appeared. This was followed seconds later by the other four members of the team.

Ged Munro was the team leader of the eight-man squad and told his men to secure the area. When secure, they looked at a way to hide the device. They spread out in four groups of two to attempting to locate a suitable place. After nine minutes, Team 3 radioed Ged that they had found an ideal area in one of the caves. The contractors had dug holes into the floor of the cave, thirty-two had been dug and fourteen had the steel supports in and surrounded by concrete. Two had the supports in, but had not been secured by concrete. The plan now was to drop the bomb into one of these two holes and cement it in with building material left by the workers. Hopefully when the contractors returned in the morning they would not realize one extra hole had been filled in. Well, why would they, he reasoned.

* * *

Fenton received a call from security that there was an old man at the main gate who wanted to speak to him and said he knew him. After hearing the name, he said he had never heard of him and told security to tell him he was busy and to go away and make an appointment like anyone else and hung up.

* * *

Ged and his team got the giant cement mixer going with what he thought should be the correct mix and poured it in. It was a race against time, as thirty-seven minutes had passed already as the last remnants of the bomb were just going under. In order to give the bomb an extra chance to pick up the signal sixty-five years later, a thin but strong copper wire ran from the detonator to the surface where Ged ensured it was attached to the steel support. He ran it inside of a lip of the support so it was not obviously visible. They now had seventeen minutes to clean up and get back to the original cave for extraction to the year 2026.

* * *

"Who was that on the phone, Fenton?" said Harry

"Oh, somebody called Ged Munro at the main gate requesting to see me urgently. I told him to make an appointment like anyone else."

Harry's face went ashen. He felt a wave of fear sweep over him. No... no, this can't be true, it's not possible, is it, he thought. He screamed, "Fenton, get back on the phone and tell security to let him in and bring him here *now!*"

* * *

Ged and his team had finished and were returning to the extraction point. They had completed the mission with four minutes to go. They entered the original cave and got into two teams of four and lay down on the dirt, and waited.

* * *

Harry stood looking out into the security pod as the old man entered the pod and was scanned. As the pod door opened he stepped into the laboratory and walked up to Harry and smiled.

"You haven't aged a bit, Mr. Stevens, unlike me. These last sixty-odd years have taken a toll on me."

* * *

The first team of four went forward in time at the exact moment the hour was up. Ged Munro and his three remaining team members lay there on the dirt of the cave floor waited for their extraction thirty seconds later. Ged's vision went blurred and then a wave of nausea swept over him. He felt like he was being pulled apart and then sprung back again over and over. He heard a scream from somewhere all around him and realized it was his own. The feeling of being everywhere and nowhere at the same time seemed to go on for an eternity and then… nothing… silence… just the sound of his laboured breathing.

He opened his eyes and found himself looking up at the cave's dimly lit ceiling. Sitting up he looked around for his three team members and immediately vomited. He sat there looking at... at something... he wasn't sure what or who. Lying next to him he saw the right side of the head of one of his team. The left side was missing and you could see the right half of his brain as it slowly slid out of the remaining part of the skull. Looking down further, he could see part of a ribcage, organs, and a leg from the knee down with an Army issue boot on the end. There was no trace at all of his other two team members.

He jumped up and ran away from the scene. Standing by the cave wall he tried to control the shock and fear that was sweeping through his mind.

* * *

"Oh, my God. Quickly, increase power to spatial navigation. Relock onto the away team and increase power," said the professor.

"Professor... look... look at the monitor!" shouted Dylan.

"Oh my God, no... no!"

Everyone in the lab looked up at the screen monitoring the time displacement area and saw what looked like one of the SAS team members, except his entire left leg and hip was missing along with both arms, left shoulder and part of his abdominal area. He lay there and managed to lift his head very slightly and looked around. Upon seeing his body, or what was left of it, he let out an ear piercing, agony-filled scream that no one in the lab would ever forget. With his eyes rolling in his sockets he tried to get up, but as he tried doing this his head rolled to the right, since the left side was not fully connected to the torso. Then there was silence. Dylan ran up the gantry as fast as he could, not really knowing what he could do when he reached the top. He looked in and saw internal organs oozing out of all the openings of the body. He was dead.

* * *

Ged Munro concentrated on controlling his breathing and attempted to think what to do next. He knew something catastrophic had happened at the lab and also knew that when they corrected that fault, they would attempt to extract him again. It did not make any difference how long it would take to correct it in their time, as long as they did it within fourteen days, but he could only stay here until the first shift started. He would have to wait lying down because if they extracted him whilst he was standing up, part of him would be rematerialized into the machine. But then if he laid there till the last moment and they did not extract him for whatever reason, then how was he going to explain to the construction team who he was? That could jeopardize the entire mission and all this would have been for nothing. So, deciding the mission was the priority, he dragged the body parts into some plastic sheeting that was lying around, and tipped them into the still wet concrete where the bomb had been placed. Then he smoothed over the surface. Standing there in his battle fatigues, he looked at his watch. It was 3:22 A.M. and he decided he would just have to try and bluff his way out when the contracting crew arrived for work. He could do a half decent American accent and they would have no reason to suspect a British Special Forces soldier would have gotten into their construction site. So he decided to just say good morning or words to that effect and just walk out. Anyway, who was going to argue with him when he had an MP5 submachine gun in his hands?

* * *

"Ged Munro, it is you, isn't it?" said Harry.

Smiling, he replied in a fake American accent, "Sure is."

Harry looked him up and down, as if to make sure all of him was there. Then he looked up at the time machine and back again and said, "What happened, did you all make it?"

Ged looked at him and with eyes that for a moment seemed to lose their shine. "No, only me."

He shook his head, looking down, and then proceeded to tell them what happened when the machine malfunctioned.

"So how did you get out? Did you get caught? Did they find the bomb?"

"As far as I know, they didn't find the bomb. As for getting out, when the first team of contractors came on duty, I just walked out. Since I was in army fatigues and armed, no one stopped me. The few U.S. Army soldiers outside barely noticed me as I got in and drove off in one of their Jeeps."

Fenton asked, "Well, what have you been doing these last sixty-six years?"

"Sixty-five years actually, and I should know, I've been counting! I managed to get back to good old Blighty a few months later and stayed out of history. I didn't want to interfere with the timelines and all that, but all that is for another day. What I want to know is what happened on this end? Did my other six guys make it?"

Harry looked at the professor and then to Ged. "The first team of four did. I'm really sorry, really I am, but no, no one made it back from the second team until now".

"Well, not intact anyway," replied Dylan.

Harry gave him a look that said to shut the fuck up. Harry asked, "If you knew the mission was going to go wrong, why didn't you tell us before today?"

"Would you have believed a ninety-two year old man who suddenly just turned up at your door and told you?"

"I might have?" said the professor.

"Yes, and that's the problem. If you had, then you might have scrubbed the mission and there would be no bomb planted. As it is, I survived and the mission was a success."

"You managed to plant it then?"

"Yes, the mission was accomplished, Mr. Harry, sir," Ged said smiling.

"Thank God, now I'll contact the PM and inform him of the success."

* * *

Josephine Cameron, head of MI5, sat in her office at Thames House video conferencing with the Prime Minister, Harry Stevens, Carol Carter, and Devon Miles in Downing Street. "Terence, I believe we can use the American spy, Lewis Rosen, to our advantage."

"How?"

"Well, as you know, although he was British born he lived most of his formative years in the U.S. and only returned here to work on the PASTec project under the direction of the CIA. Therefore, his loyalty to the state is America. From our informants within the CIA, he has been promised a glittering career as head of their time machine program, which of course, would be our stolen program.

We propose to place him into a safe house with two of our agents after feeding him some misinformation. We then let him escape and give him a chance to contact his CIA operative here to supply the said information."

"What misinformation are you going to give our Mr. Rosen?" said Devon.

"Tell him that the time machine is up and running and working perfectly. Say that the Americans will have to back off otherwise past events will, how should I say, catch up with them."

"You are referring to the little device in a certain mountain range?" replied Harry.

"Well, yes, and others. We feed him lots of red herrings then when NORAD goes bang they will believe the others."

"Sounds good to me," replied Terence, "That should keep them on the back foot. If they don't back down, then we keep going back in time and continually destroy parts of their economy, infrastructure, and way of life. With a time machine we can go where we like, when we like, and do it to who we like as often as we like. In fact we can even go back and kill Leonard Cain before he becomes president. We will change history to suit ourselves, if need be. The difference being between the Americans and us is that we want to use it for the betterment of mankind, unlike the Yanks who want it for themselves for absolute power and wealth over every other country on Earth.

* * *

Lewis Rosen was taken from his holding cell at Thames House at approximately 4:30 P.M. on Thursday, three and a half days after being detained by MI5. He hadn't showered and was still in the same clothes. He was starting to smell. "Where are you taking me? I have rights, you know"

"We're taken you somewhere where you can wash and change, you smelly bastard," replied Craig Stanton, "Now get in the car."

Lewis was then pushed into the rear seat of the Vauxhall and handcuffed to the door handle. Craig and his associate MI5 agent Mark Atkins got into the front and with Mark at the wheel drove off to the safe house. After ten minutes, they pulled into a rough Council estate where the safe house was situated. The plan was that in the night the guard that was looking after him would pretend to accidentally fall asleep, giving Lewis the chance to escape.

"Mark, keep driving, I think we might have a tail on us. A black Ford Avenger has been behind us for the last three minutes."

Mark, Craig, and Lewis were just approaching a T-junction when the car following suddenly sped up. Mark increased his speed and went right at the junction at that same moment another car came from the right at about sixty miles per hour and rammed straight into the side of the Vauxhall. All the airbags exploded at once and with a sickening sound of crumpled steel and smashing glass, the Vauxhall slid sideways into the curb. It took Craig a few seconds for his head to clear and he looked across at his friend, Mark. The whole driver's side door had folded in onto the driver's seat and Mark had been severely injured. Blood was pumping out of a severed artery in his thigh and hitting the now twisted steering wheel. Blood was also streaming from a large wound on his head and he was unconscious. He tried to open his passenger side door but it would not open since it had jammed due to the twisted wreckage he was now trapped in. Then he was aware of two men, one standing at his shattered side window and another at the rear door. Thinking they were passersby, he shouted at them to call for help, but they just stood there. Then he was aware of a gun pointing in through the shattered window and heard two thudded shots. He saw his friend Mark grunt and fall forward. Then the gun was pointed at him and he saw him pull the trigger.

The two CIA agents walked around the smashed car. While one went to the front and fired four shots into the front cabin, the other wrenched open the rear door and pulled the rear passenger out. The agent realized the man's left hand was handcuffed to the door handle. He fired at the door panel connected to the handle and the door handle disintegrated, releasing him. The agent pushed him into the Avenger, and along with the driver of the car that crashed into the Vauxhall, drove off at top speed.

* * *

The President was in a meeting with all of his senior advisors in the White House when his phone rang. He picked it up and said, "Hello, Cain here."

"Mr. President, David Stack here."

David Stack was the head of overseas operations for the CIA. "I've just been informed about an asset who had been removed by MI5, Lewis Rosen. We had him at the British PASTec complex and he has been released by three CIA agents at approximately 11:45 A.M. GMT."

"Excellent. What can he tell us? Has he got any information on the progress of the time machine or what the Brits intend to do?"

"Yes, sir, he certainly does. He said that the Brits are using the machine to change past events to their advantage today. Also, they can destroy most of our military at will."

"What's that supposed to mean?"

"It means that, if you believe them, the Brits for the first time seem to have the upper hand."

* * *

"Shit, they're both dead!"

Josephine replied, "Yes, Terry, each was shot once in the head and once in the chest."

"And Lewis, the spy?"

"He's gone. He was taken by the CIA we presume."

"Well, at least that part went according to plan. Mr. Rosen will be giving them all the red herrings we fed him, though we just lost two field agents in the process."

* * *

"Harry, until the fault is corrected, the time machine is offline. We cannot afford to lose anyone else until it's fixed," said the professor.

"Well, how long is that?" asked Harry

"Are you taking the piss? How the fuck do I know? We don't even know what's wrong with it, and we need to know that before we can fix it."

"How long before you know what's wrong then?"

"Oh, give me strength."

CHAPTER 5

Friday, 6:59 A.M., Day 5

Captain Kip Jarvis was on the bridge of the Lexington. He leaned on the gray steel window frame and looked up at the leaden gray sky. The dull, drab colour reminded him of the ships of his strike group. The wind was blowing at eighteen knots and the sea had a gentle swell.

The carrier strike group sailed into British waters and headed for the English Channel. They had made good time across the Atlantic and had been lucky with the weather. Now they were just seven hours from Portsmouth. Reconnaissance from U.S. spy satellites in geostationary orbit above the British Isles caught the Royal Navy attempting to intercept them. Kip Jarvis had to be careful. The Royal Navy's battle fleet approaching was a very potent force, and although not as powerful, was still closely matched with his own. He also had to be aware that he was in enemy waters and the Brits had the advantage to bring in more ships quickly if needed. They also had air support from the R.A.F. from land bases in Britain and across the channel in France. If things really did kick off, the Brits could ask the French to help and would probably get it. The U.S. was not that popular around the world due to its sometimes chaotic

91

foreign policy over the last thirty years or so.

He had been given this mission to extract some Brits from a complex fifty-odd miles inland and to destroy it after getting the plans for a new machine that would be world changing. That's all he had been told. He knew there was more to it, but he was only being told what they thought he needed to know. Normally that would have been okay, but since being given the orders to basically attack the U.K., America's staunchest ally and closest friend, this just did not feel right. He had relatives who lived there, for Christ's sake. It felt like he was attacking them, too. His feeling of foreboding since setting sail had gotten stronger as the fleet had gotten closer to British waters.

•

* * *

The Royal Navy's battle fleet was heading in the same direction in the Channel as the American carrier group, but just at eight knots though. The fleet admiral, Sir Roger Penrose, was on the Royal Navy's most powerful warship ever, which was also the Navy's flagship, the HMS Queen Elizabeth, nicknamed Queenie. He was waiting for the U.S. fleet to catch up so the Royal Navy could escort them to the Navy's home base. The Prime Minister had informed him of the PASTec project and the U.S.'s intentions. He was not going to give them room to try anything, with ships and submarines around and under their fleet; he intended to deter the Americans from doing whatever they came for. If not, then he was determined to stop them with whatever force was necessary. After all, his ship's motto was *quodlibet quod necese* ("whatever it takes").

On the bridge of the Queen Elizabeth carrier, the Admiral was standing with John Stewart and the radio operator in the radio communications section. "Right, so if things start to get a bit lively, you want me to contact the American fleet commander, er, what's his name? Skip Jarvis?" said John.

"No… Kip Jarvis, you plonker."

"Watch your language, phones," replied the Admiral.

"Sorry, sir," replied the grinning radio operator.

"Right, and as the President I'm to give him some confusing and conflicting orders, giving us an advantage, an edge in any altercation that might occur."

"Yeah, you got it, Mr. Impersonator."

The things I do for King and country, John mused.

* * *

King Charles, Camilla, Princes William and Harry, and respective wives Katharine and Helen, along with their children were just taking off from the Ascension Islands en route to Australia in total secrecy in two separate Nimrod aircraft with four Typhoon fighter jets escorting them, along with a refuelling aircraft. The royal family was spread out amongst the two, in case one crashed, so that at least some of the royal family would survive. Princes William and Harry were both set against leaving Great Britain. Being both military men, it felt like they were running away when they should be there to fight for their country like everyone else. However the Prime Minister and the heads of the military, along with all their aides, were insistent and had said no.

Prince William looked up at his father as the plane left the tarmac and said, "I wonder if we will ever return, and if we do, what type of country we will be returning to?"

King Charles was surprisingly nimble and alert for a seventy-eight year old and looked up at his son and replied. "I'm sure we will return, son, those green pastures will still be there waiting for you, Will. I cannot believe the Americans would be so stupid."

"I'm not so sure, father. Times are so different now: overpopulation, meagre food supply, dwindling energy reserves, such imbalances in wealth from one nation to another, natural resources depleted, crime, and corruption. It seems problems arise faster that we can solve them."

Charles looked at his son and wished he could be more sure, but deep down, he knew Will was right. The world was changing. This was a pivotal moment in history and he had a feeling he would never step foot on British soil again.

* * *

Professor Jones and his team had been working on the problem for three days now, but still wasn't sure if they had sorted the problem out. It hadn't helped that the Defence Secretary kept pressuring them for a positive result all the time. Dylan had the idea that instead of letting the time machine take whatever power it wanted to run, they would calculate the energy needed for a time slip and then limit it to that so there was no excess energy being stored within the wormhole. They also inserted an energy limiter that automatically controlled the energy usage to predefined limits. They decided to run it in neutral, neutral being the formation of a wormhole but not sending anything back or forward in time, to see how it operated. If all went okay then the lab would send something inanimate through time and see if it worked as calculated.

Harry asked, "Right, how's it going? Has the power issue been resolved?"

Dylan replied, "We think its okay now. We've run it four times and managed to control the power usage to what it just needs for time travel only. However, there is still the excess energy still stored within the wormhole from previous runs, but we think that's manageable."

"Right, what shall we send?" said Fenton.

"Let's send my cheese sandwich that's on my desk five minutes forward in time," replied Dylan grinning.

With the sandwich placed inside the time displacement area, the coordinates were fed into the computer. The machine began to hum again, though this time there was not so much of a tingling feeling on the skin. The wormhole formed, and then the sandwich blurred and disappeared.

"Okay, switch off power," said Dylan.

The power shut down immediately. "Shutdown seemed fine that time, professor" said Harry.

"Yes, seems okay this time," replied Fenton.

Exactly five minutes after dematerializing, the sandwich re-materialised on Dylan's desk looking no worse for wear. Dylan picked it up and took a mouthful. "Tastes fine to me, nicely matured, in fact."

"Great, I'll inform the PM that we're up and running now," said Harry.

"Well, I wouldn't go that far. That was just one test; we still need to do more testing to be sure."

"Well, you keep testing. I've got to get back to London now."

* * *

Kip Jarvis was on the bridge of the USS Lexington looking at the radar image in front of him at eight blips. Each indicated a Royal Navy warship. The American carrier strike group was in formation just eight miles from them. The information he had received from their spy satellites told him he had two British super carriers, four frigates, and two destroyers approaching. Sonar was trying to trace the nuclear subs which he knew must be there as well.

The officer in charge of navigation turned to Commander Jarvis. "Sir, the Royal Navy is doing eight knots. Do you want us to slow to their speed or continue on at our current speed of twenty-four knots?"

Kip thought for a few seconds. "No, continue at our current speed. Let's keep the Brits on the hop, and let them follow us to their home port."

* * *

Admiral Penrose watched on the radar screen and also film from a Nimrod spy plane flying over the American strike group who were now just three nautical miles behind them. He said, "It looks like they are not slowing. They are going to continue on at their current speed of twenty-four knots. At this rate they will catch up and overtake us in minutes, leaving us to catch up in our home waters. Well, that's not going to happen, let's see how they deal with this."

Penrose ordered all eight Royal Navy ships that were sailing in an arrowhead formation to immediately turn ninety degrees to port and to stop. The maneuver effectively blocked the American strike group from proceeding without taking evasive action to avoid colliding with the British fleet.

* * *

"What the fuck are those Brits doing? Christ almighty, order the carrier group to veer to starboard immediately. Tell them to reduce speed *now!*" screamed the American commander.

* * *

Admiral Penrose watched the situation very closely. He knew this maneuver was extremely dangerous and that his ships would come off worse if the Americans continued at their current speed and course, eighty thousand tons of metal from a carrier coming at you at twenty-four knots slicing broadside into a destroyer of eight thousand tons. It doesn't take a mathematician to work out who would come off worst. He was banking on their strike group commander reacting immediately to avoid a collision. Radar showed that they were taking evasive action and slowing. Penrose then ordered his fleet to turn immediately to starboard ninety degrees to bring them back on their original course.

* * *

The U.S. carrier strike group was in disarray, some had turned forty-five degrees and other smaller ships had managed to turn ninety degrees. However, the Lexington itself had hardly managed to turn more than ten degrees in the time. Now the Brits were turning back on course, leaving his strike group to reform and catch up.

* * *

Admiral Penrose let out a deep sigh of relief that this highly risky maneuver worked. He now ordered his battle fleet to spread out in formation to stop any U.S. ships from overtaking and ordered the fleet to speed up to twenty-six knots. Let the Yanks do the bloody chasing for once, thought Penrose.

* * *

"Bloody hell, that was close. What the fuck, I've never seen a maneuver like that. Their commander is either as brave as hell or absolutely stupid. At this moment, I don't know which."

Commander Kip Jarvis shouted to his officers around him, "Get this strike group back in formation and catch up with the Limeys."

The U.S. carrier strike group returned into formation and started to follow the British battle group that was now about ten nautical miles ahead. After nearly an hour, the American group had managed to catch up with the British fleet, but only after accelerating to thirty knots. "Okay, match their speed and course. Keep us one nautical mile behind them," ordered Jarvis.

* * *

"Dylan, we need to test again with live tissue. I want you to send me back. I want you to send me back to 2011, the day man discovered the Higgs boson particle at the Large Hadron Collider," said the professor.

"Why? Why then?"

"Why not? It needs to be tested. I've got to go some time, so why not there? I know I get there safely since we all saw me there the other day. So as I've never been there, then this must be that time-line?"

"Oh right, that make sense," replied Dylan. "But how do you know that this is then, couldn't that then be later and this is not it now?"

"Shut it. Dyl, you're even confusing me!"

* * *

Leonard Cain was sitting in the White House Situation Room along with Vice President Richard Novak, and all his Joint Chiefs of Staff, along with the Director of the CIA, John Stack. "So, what have we got? Situation report, guys?"

Admiral Cartwright spoke first. "Well, the Brits pulled a blinder today."

He proceeded to inform them of the events in the English Channel with the Royal Navy.

"Is the raid on PASTec still on?" asked the President.

"Yes, sir."

"Anything else I should know about?"

The Vice President looked up and said, "I think we may have a problem developing with the media. They're not stupid. They know something big is happening. They just don't know what."

"Yet," said John Stack.

"What do you mean, yet? It's your job to stop them from finding out."

"Easier said, than done. The longer this goes on and the bigger it gets, they're bound to find out sooner or later."

"Well, it better be later, so you better see to it, John."

* * *

"Okay, Dylan, are you ready?" asked Fenton.

"Are you sure about this, prof?"

"No!"

"Fair enough."

The machine hummed and the professor's form blurred on the screen and then vanished.

* * *

Fenton's vision blurred for a second or so and then cleared. He found himself lying down in the storeroom that they had selected. He stood up and felt sick while he looked around.

Fantastic, he thought. Even though he'd designed it and had sent others through time before now, the fact that he'd now travelled through time somehow made it more real. They had researched before sending him back as to what identification the scientists in 2011 were wearing at the Large Hadron Collider. The technicians had had one made that gave him unlimited access.

He also had decided to stay at the Large Hadron Collider for twelve hours, partly to test the machine, as no one had stayed that long in time so far and also so that he could have a good look around.

Wearing a white open-necked shirt, his identification badge was clipped to his dark trousers and his glasses sat on the end of his nose under his thinning and greying hair. He walked out of the closet and strode along the corridors to the main machine room where the

Collider was situated. Prior to the time slip back to the CERN complex, he had taken the time to study the layout of the building and the location of personnel so he would not arouse suspicion. There was also one member of staff he especially wanted to see.

* * *

"Where's the professor?" enquired Harry.

"He gone on a little trip," replied Dylan.

"Trip? A little trip, at a time like this? Where's he gone?"

Dylan looked up at the time machine and nodded in its direction. "There!"

"Oh for fuck's sake, no, tell me you're taking the piss?"

"'Fraid not."

"And what happens if something happens to him and we need him on this side of time?"

"His choice, Harry. He designed most of it. He's given the best part of his life to it. It needed to be tested, so why shouldn't he?"

Harry had no answer.

* * *

Both fleets were anchored off the coast of southern England, east of the Isle of Wight and overlooked the British naval port of Portsmouth. Two more Royal Navy Type-45 destroyers exited the naval base and reinforced the already strong flotilla anchored in the Solent.

* * *

Kip Jarvis ordered his carrier group to anchor just off the coast of England, five miles from the British naval base at Portsmouth.

Aboard his ship, preparations were underway to get the Chinooks checked, armed, and fuelled ready for their incursion into British air space and the attack on the PASTec complex later that night. The one-hundred-and-forty Green Berets were checking and rechecking their equipment and going over the raid details in readiness for the mission. Kip leaned on the gray steel frame of the bridge window, and looked over the coast of Portsmouth. He could see through his binoculars hundreds of people standing on the beach and promenade with binoculars and cameras of their own looking and taking pictures of this amazing sight of British and American naval might moored just a few miles from their shores.

The Spinnaker observation tower, which overlooked the Solent, was crammed full of people trying to get a better vantage point. Small speedboats and yachts tried to come close to the two battle groups, but were being kept at bay by both British and American patrol boats.

He had received numerous calls from the local media and town hall officials for interviews and queries as to why no members of crew had disembarked to enjoy the sights and sounds the city had to offer. He found himself feeling guilty. He knew that in a few short hours he would give the order to send in a squad of Special Forces to attack an unarmed complex and kill potentially hundreds of British people. His feeling of foreboding grew and grew as time went on.

* * *

Admiral Sir Roger Penrose, Commander of the British battle fleet, sat with his officers in his situation room on HMS Queen Elizabeth.

"So, it looks like they're still intending to carry out the attack on PASTec. GCHQ has intercepted signals from the American carrier strike group and NORAD that confirm it's still a go for the raid tonight."

"Sir, why don't we just shoot them down as soon as they take off?" said one of his junior lieutenants.

"Simple, lieutenant, if we shoot as soon as they take off, we will look like the bad guys. Besides it is too highly populated right here on the coast, whereas inland over woods in the countryside at night, no one should see or get injured except them."

"Sir, we've managed to trace on sonar three of the four American subs. It's proven difficult as they have been using stealth technology to hide their position. We also know from G.C.H.Q. from communications to NORAD that they have so far only detected one of our three subs."

"Good, things seem to be turning in our favor now. Let's hope that luck continues!"

* * *

Professor Fenton Jones had an ulterior motive in going through time to the 2011 CERN physics research center. His ex-wife was working there as an administrator before he met her at that time and he wanted to see her again even though she wouldn't know who he was. She had been his liaison officer at the very beginning of the PASTec. program and helped him access all the information and results of the Higgs boson experiment that led to the foundation of the time machine project.

There were so many people working in and around the CERN

Institute that another face in the crowd didn't seem out of place and as he had an identification card with full access, no one gave him a second glance. Fortunately, he knew what he was talking about if he was asked. He did not know the location of where she worked so he thought he would hang around the staff restaurant and hopefully she would come in for lunch.

He sat there for two and a half hours and ended up eating two meals so as not to arouse suspicion, but she never turned up. Damn, he thought, I'll have to wait until dinner later this afternoon.

Wondering through the massive complex was amazing. The sheer size and magnitude of the machine even dwarfed his time machine. He wandered around looking and nodding at other staff and making small chat when needed. He stood behind a control panel as the scientists activated the Large Hadron Collider to detect this previously unknown quantum particle. He stood there for about ten minutes when he felt a slight tingling sensation all over his skin. It lasted only a few seconds and then was gone, only to feel it again about ten to twelve seconds later.

It wasn't until a couple of minutes later after feeling tingly that he put the two and two together and realized that this must be the moment that he had seen earlier in the lab.

He wandered around for nearly four more hours, giving advice here and there to some of the scientists as to how they could accomplish this or that. Though he had to be careful, one scientist got so excited at a calculation he gave that it brought him unwanted attention; so he quickly made an excuse to leave. Heading back to the restaurant for dinner, he walked up a flight of stairs and he looked up as she was coming down, holding a black book binder in her left hand. There she was, his future wife to be, with her long wavy dark hair, brown eyes, Spanish suntanned skin, and slender figure. She was dressed in a tight mid-length skirt and a primrose-colored blouse. She looked stunningly beautiful, just as he remembered her. When he looked straight into her eyes, a wave of emotion went coursing through him—feelings that he had forgotten he had since she left him all those years ago. He found himself just standing there staring, on the stairs with his mouth open, and blocking her path.

"Excuse me, sir. Sir? Hello? Anyone in?" she said, looking at him.

"Oh, sorry, I was miles away. My name's Fenton. Professor Fenton Jones."

"Hi, my name's Cl—"

"Claire. Yes, I know."

"You do, do you? Well, that's nice. You must have a good memory, what with all the people who work here. Even I cannot remember everyone's names."

"Would you like to come to dinner with me?" asked Fenton.

Standing there and looking him up and down, she raised her left eyebrow. "Well, you certainly don't waste time, do you? Most professors aren't that forward in asking for a date."

"Oh no, sorry. I meant the canteen here."

"Right," she said slowly, nodding her head up and down gently. "So you don't want to take me out for dinner, then?" she asked with a smile.

"No, yes, oh, crikey!"

Claire stood there smiling at this funny man she had never seen before.

"Okay, you can take me out to the canteen to start with."

"Great…er, now?"

"Now will be fine."

* * *

Two Chinooks took off from the Lexington and the other two from the Enterprise. Each helicopter had thirty-five Green Berets aboard. They were flying over the city of Portsmouth at 10:45 P.M. It was a perfectly clear still night. Even with the light pollution from the city, you could still see many stars.

The estimated time of arrival to the mission target was nineteen minutes. Flying straight and low at five hundred feet ensured that they cleared Portsdown hill three miles inland. The mission commander expected the British to attempt contact or even follow them, but no, nothing. If the situation was reversed he was sure he would be curious as to where a group of foreign helicopters were flying to over his homeland. If the Brits were this lax, then they deserved all they got, he thought.

The four Chinooks flew in single-line formation, two hundred feet from each other and all in radio silence. Radio contact was to be used only in an emergency. Each chopper was fitted with stealth features to reduce its radar signature. Also, each Chinook's rotor audio signature had been reduced by thirty percent. Being painted completely black, the helicopters were almost invisible to the naked eye at night.

Looking out one of the windows at the open countryside, the Special Forces' commander could see almost nothing except for the odd light dotted here and there. They were probably farmhouses or the odd country cottage, he thought. Suddenly a bright flash came from somewhere in the woods down below and all hell broke out. An enormous explosion came from behind them and he saw one of the Chinooks fall out of the sky in a ball of flames. Suddenly, another flash came from the ground and another explosion came from behind while another helicopter went down in flames.

Radio contact was established from his chopper to the one other remaining Chinook, and he ordered evasive action, and to fly as low as possible to prevent the Brits getting a clear lock on them. After a minute they had cleared the woods below and were flying over a small town that according to his satellite navigation was called Petersfield.

Now that the element of surprise had gone and obviously the Brits knew what they intended to do, the Mission Commander contacted the Lexington for further instructions. Was the mission scrubbed or was it still a go with the remaining two helicopters?

Kip Jarvis sat in the command chair on the bridge of the Lexington with a mug of hot black unsweetened coffee in his left hand. Sleep eluded him. It just did not feel right. The Brits must have seen the Chinooks leave the two carriers and head inland, so why didn't they contact the Lexington and ask where they were headed? Why didn't they follow them? It just did not feel right and the feeling of foreboding he had felt since he had left Norfolk Naval Station days earlier was still with him.

The radio operator sitting at his station on the bridge suddenly sat bolt upright and was listening to his headphones. "Sir, we have a problem, the mission commander is reporting two Chinooks were shot down and the remaining two took evasive action. He is requesting instructions: is the mission still a go or scrubbed?"

Jumping down from his command chair, he strode quickly to the radio station. "Fuck, get more info. Ask him what happened?"

The radio operator spoke quickly into his microphone and then said, "Sir, two Chinooks were shot down over woods near town of Petersfield. The remaining two are undamaged and continuing on to target. He's requesting instructions: is mission still a go now that the Brits know what were up to, or do we scrub?"

"Shit, scrub. Scrub the mission. Get 'em back here ASAP"

"Yes sir," said the radio operator who spoke quickly again into his microphone. "Abort mission, repeat, abort mission. Return to base, repeat, return to base. These are the orders of Commander Kip Jarvis. Repeat, return to base, mission aborted."

* * *

Onboard the two remaining Chinooks, they heard the order to return and both pilots started to turn the choppers about when another flash came from another wooded area below. Suddenly, an enormous fireball erupted one hundred feet behind the mission commander's chopper.

"Fucking hell, they're firing on us again. Contact the Lexington and inform them we are under attack again over the woods near the town of Liss."

Aboard the Lexington the radio operator received the update that a third Chinook was down. "Christ, what a fuck up. Tell the remaining pilot to get back here as fast as he can," said Jarvis.

"Yes, sir," replied the radio operator.

Kip was watching the operator speak to the one remaining

chopper when the operator's face went white. "Come in, chopper one. Repeat, come in, chopper one. Come in, over."

He looked up at his commanding officer and said, "Sir, chopper one is gone, too".

* * *

Terence Summerfield, Harry Stevens, Devon Miles, and General Sir Stirling Davenport, and the Home Secretary Carol Carter were all sitting in the cabinet room of Number 10, watching events unfold live right in front of them. They watched as each American Chinook was shot down over the English countryside. As the fourth and final one went down, Carol said to no one in particular, "Well, the shit is going to hit the fan now. We've just escalated the tension up two notches."

"Don't know about two notches," replied the Prime Minister. He looked at the General and said,

"Give the order to detonate the nuclear device under NORAD."

"Yes, sir."

The General picked up the phone in front of him and spoke to the M.O.D. Satellite Command Center based in North Wales. "This is General Sir Stirling Davenport, Chief of the Defence Staff. Execute Project Trojan Horse, code three-three-one-zero."

He nodded and passed the handset to the Prime Minister. "This is the Prime Minister. Execute Project Trojan Horse, code three-one-seven-three-zero."

On the other end, the Prime Minister heard the confirmed reply code, "Executing command zero-zero-zero."

The Prime Minister replaced the receiver and looked around the room, "Well, the shit certainly will hit the fan now. We've just ratcheted it up to more like twenty notches."

* * *

The U.S. President, Vice President Richard Novak, David Stack—the head of overseas CIA Operations—and Admiral Cartwright were all sitting in the Situation Room of the White House watching the events unfold over the gentle, rolling English Hampshire hills over 3,000 miles away.

Leonard Cain sat there for what seemed like minutes staring at the spy satellite image in front of him. He watched the burning inferno, and he knew that he had just witnessed the deaths of one hundred and forty brave American men and women.

One of the phones rang. "Mr. President, I've just had confirmation from the carrier strike group Commander in the English Channel. We have lost all the Special Forces assets en route to the PASTec. complex. They were all shot down by the British military. The strike group Commander Kip Jarvis is requesting instructions," said Admiral Cartwright.

Leonard just sat there staring at the back of his hands for thirty seconds, and looked up. "How the *fuck* did those Limeys know what we intended to do and where?"

"Mr. President, the only way they could have known is they must have a spy in our administration," said Richard Novak.

"You're forgetting one thing, Rich," replied Admiral Cartwright. "They have a time machine. If that is operational, then anything we do now in the present time can be compromised. They see an action we take, and they can then go back and change it to suit themselves. For all we know our raid could have been successful in one timeline, but then changed so we are now all living in an altered time line. But, we'll never know."

Another one of the phones rang on the desk in front of where they were sitting. The Vice President picked it up and his mouth fell open. His face went ashen and he dropped the phone onto the desk and looked at the President with wide eyes, and said in a shaky voice, "Mr. President."

"What is it, Richard?" said Leonard, looking at him with a growing sense of dread.

"Mr President, NORAD's gone"

"Gone? Gone? What do you mean, gone?"

"Just that. We're getting reports that NORAD and part of the Cheyenne mountain range has gone."

"What? You mean an earthquake?"

"No, sir. It's been nuked. The Brits have just nuked us. They've just taken out our air defence command center."

Everyone just sat there, not quite believing what they had just heard. The President said, "How the hell did they get a nuclear device past all our defences? Surely we would have seen it coming?"

The Admiral looked up again and said, "You're all forgetting what I said just now. They have a time machine. They can do what they like, when they like. That asset, Lewis Rosen, who we had in the PASTec. program and managed to extract from MI5 the other day said that the British could wipe out our military at will, but we didn't take it that seriously. We thought the Brits might have been feeding him misinformation. It seems we were wrong. But how could a small island nation like Britain, with limited resources, take on the military might of the U.S.?"

"Well, it looks like they can and have," replied the President,

"Mr. President, the carrier strike group commander is still on the phone awaiting instructions."

* * *

At 11:40 P.M., John Stewart was still in the radio control room of the Q.E. Carrier withAdmiral Penrose awaiting instructions for misdirecting the American strike group by impersonating the U.S. President. "Sir, we've managed to intercept messages to and from the U.S. carrier strike group and the White House," said Phones, the radio operator.

"Excellent, Phones. Good work. Can you link in on their encryption wavelength so when we speak to them they will think it's the White House?" replied the Admiral.

"Believe so, sir, I believe so."

* * *

Fenton was sitting opposite from Claire in one of the staff canteens at CERN. He had the advantage of knowing quite a lot about her, because of their previous relationship. However, it hadn't happened yet in this time, so she knew nothing about it. She was amazed that he seemed to be so in tune with what she liked and disliked. He appeared so intuitive. She thought it felt like she had known him for years, which made her feel so relaxed in his company.

Fenton sat there looking at this beautiful woman and couldn't but help love her. He remembered the first day they had met, almost fourteen years ago, or next year, depending on which time line you're coming from.

The Research and Development section of the Ministry of Defence approached Fenton to lead a project that could quite literary change the future. Claire had been assigned as his liaison officer between the Large Hadron Collider project and his time machine program and a relationship developed quite quickly at that time.

Two years later they were married. It was only due to the ever-increasing pressure of the time machine project that ended up putting more pressure on their marriage until finally she had had enough that caused her to leave. He couldn't blame her. He was hardly ever at home and he often slept at the complex for days on end. It was inevitable that she would leave. He was surprised she stayed as long as she did. Now, the only difference was he was fifteen years older now than when they previously first met in the following year. He also hadn't looked after himself as well as he should have, so he guessed she probably didn't find him as attractive as she did when she first met him.

"You're not eating much, Fenty. You'll waste away."

Fenton was having trouble eating three meals in six hours. He was also amazed that she had called him Fenty within thirty minutes of meeting him. It had been her pet name for him in their previous future relationship.

"I've got some hours owing to me and I was going to take tomorrow afternoon off. You're more than welcome to take me out for a proper dinner then?"

"Oh right, really, um, I'm not sure if I'm going to be around by then."

"Oh! Where you off to then? Don't tell me you can't find time for me in your busy schedule?"

He knew it was wrong and he should be thinking of getting back to the future, but looking across the table and seeing her again made him pause. Knowing that she still liked him even as an older man and knowing that it was his work that lost her before in the future, he decided to say yes.

She handed him her card with her address on it. "Okay, you can pick me up at 7 P.M. tomorrow night—and don't be late."

"Yes, I know you don't like people who are late."

"Yes, you're right. I don't like people who don't arrive on time— but how did you know?"

He smiled. "Just an intuitive guess."

Claire stood up and picked up her folder. "Until tomorrow, then."

She walked around the table and kissed him gently on the cheek. With that, she walked away, saying, "Remember, 7 P.M.," and was gone.

* * *

Fenton laid down in the storeroom ready for the time shift back to 2026. He had sat down in the restroom earlier and thought through what had happened. Now lying on the floor, all of a sudden his vision blurred and he was back in the future. He felt a bit nauseous as he climbed down the gantry and walked up to Dylan and said, "What's new, Dyl?"

"Christ, you go off in time for twelve hours and all this shit happens."

He proceeded to tell Fenton what had transpired with the

downed helicopters and NORAD and the stand off between the two carrier groups in the Channel. "Is the machine working okay? When I rematerialized just then, I felt a bit sick."

"No, we're starting to get power fluctuations again."

"I thought we installed some power regulators to prevent this?"

"We did, but it's happening again"

As Fenton walked out of the lab, he said, "Well, I'll leave it with you, chaps. I'm popping off home."

Dylan watched him go and thought he looked rather preoccupied. Normally, the professor would have got straight down with everyone else and tried to work out the problem. Obviously something had happened while he had been gone.

* * *

Leonard Cain had discussed his options with his senior military advisors and the Vice President regarding the carrier group's next move and their response to the NORAD attack. It had been decided that the carrier group should remain in place. The White House had been outraged by the act of aggression on American soil and the total destruction of the NORAD complex. The Americans also were fuming at the deaths of the Special Forces troops and over seven hundred military personnel who had been working in and around NORAD.

Considering that the carrier strike group was off the coast of Britain, if the U.S. decided to retaliate, the strike group was exactly where they wanted it.

* * *

On board the Queen Elizabeth, Phones had overheard the transmission to the U.S. carrier group to remain in place. He immediately reported this to Admiral Penrose. "Right, John, time for you to go to work. This is what I want you to say…"

* * *

John said, "Commander Kip Jarvis, this is the President of the United States. There has been a new development that I cannot discuss over the radio. I am giving you new orders that are to be obeyed explicitly without question—I repeat, *without* question—do you understand?"

"Yes, Mr. President."

"You must be aware of the nuclear strike against U.S. soil. Well, your orders are to return back to the Norfolk naval station immediately. You and your carrier strike group are also ordered to maintain complete communication silence during the entire return voyage. We believe some or all our communications might have been compromised by Britain's GCHQ. You will contact the other ships in your strike group only by Morse code, only then if it is deemed urgent. Do you understand these instructions clearly?

"Yes, Mr. President, crystal clear."

"Good luck, and may God be with us all."

Looking up at John, Phones said, "Do you know, matey, you're really quite good."

The Admiral just smiled at the pair and went off to bed nodding his head.

CHAPTER 6

Fenton went into his bedroom and picked out a shirt and trousers that Claire had bought him years ago and laid them out on the bed. He showered, shaved, and got dressed. He stood in front of the mirror and looked at himself.

"Not bad, still fits and looks quite good" he thought. Then, sitting in the arm chair by the bay window that looked out over the open countryside, he started to think about the events of the past five days. The danger the country was now in and the deaths on both sides were all due to his time machine. Events had gone by so fast he hardly had had time to think of the enormous consequences. Now sitting here in the seclusion and calm of his cottage, he began thinking of another way, what if he went back in time to 2011 and stayed? He could start his relationship again with Claire, but armed with the foreknowledge of future events in both his professional and personal life. This time he could balance his work and his private life so as not to lose her again. This time, he could build the time machine with multiple governments involved, just like the CERN project; so no one solely had control, so the whole world would benefit equally, not just one country.

He sat there looking across the open fields for over an hour. He thought about what he could do. Then he leaned forward and picked up a framed photo of Claire from the window ledge. He sat and stared at the image of her smiling face and remembered all those happy times together. He drew in a deep breath. He breathed out and placed the picture back down, stood, turned, and packed a large case of clean clothes and assorted items. He walked out of the cottage and drove into Crookham Village just over two miles away. He entered the small bank and walked up to the foreign exchange counter. He handed over his biometric debit card and asked for ten thousand Euros. The cashier counted out the money and placed it into an envelope and handed it to him along with his card. He returned to his car and drove to the lab.

As he went through the usual security checks, he realized that this would be the last time he'd do this. He thought, well in this time line, anyway. He walked up to Dylan. "Hi, Dyl, do me a favor and send me back to the same year as yesterday, but eighteen hours later. I've got here the exact time and location coordinates."

Dylan looked up with a quizzical look on his face, "What… why? You're dressed a bit smart, aren't you," and starting to smile he said, "What are you up to? What's with the suitcase?" He handed Dylan the new coordinates. "Oh, nothing really. I've just got a bit of unfinished business I want to attend to."

As he started to walk up the gantry, he turned and looked straight into his friend's eyes. "See you later. Or is it sooner? Well, whatever. Goodbye, mate, be seeing you."

He climbed the ladder and lay down in the time displacement area with the suitcase next to him and waited. Dylan spoke into the intercom and said, "Prof, how long do you want to be gone?"

"Make it twelve hours," knowing that he would not be at the extraction location in twelve hours.

"Okay, see you soon."

Dylan directed the technicians to bring all the systems online for time slip and then the professor was gone. He sat there looking up at where the professor had been a moment ago and thought that the professor seemed a bit distant. What unfinished business could he have, he thought? Then all the alarms went off in the lab. "Sod it, the bloody machine's pulling more energy again and it won't shut down!" said Dylan to no-one in particular.

* * *

The American carrier strike group headed west at thirty knots along the English Channel towards the Atlantic Ocean and the open sea. The Pentagon was continually attempting to contact them, but as ordered by the President himself, he ignored all attempts at communication, knowing that their transmissions could be compromised.

Kip could not believe NORAD was gone—destroyed by the Brits—but then we were going to attack one of their installations on mainland Britain, he thought. "Damn, I wish I knew what all this was really about; the Brits would not have destroyed NORAD without a bloody good reason. What the hell was his government up to?"

* * *

The British Prime Minister sat in the White Drawing Room of

Number 10 Downing Street. Sitting opposite was his wife, Kimberly. The Prime Minister had a glass of whisky in his left hand and stared at the painting over the fireplace of old London town with St. Paul's Cathedral in the background.

"Terry, you okay? You've not said much in the last hour or so."

She got up from the chair opposite and sat down next to him. Sipping a glass of dry white wine in her right hand, she placed her left hand over his right and squeezed gently. He carried on looking at that picture without saying anything for another full minute before turning to look at her. She saw tears welling up in his eyes and saw the pain and anguish registered in them. "What have I done, Kim? I've ordered the deaths of hundreds, maybe thousands, of people. I've used the first nuclear weapon since the second World War in anger."

"What could you have done? You were backed into a corner. They were threatening us with the same. What were you supposed to do?"

"But I personally ordered their deaths. I'm responsible for that."

"That goes with the territory, Terry. They kept pushing and threatening. What did they expect you to do? Just hand over the greatest invention of all time without any resistance? They started this and you've hopefully finished it."

"I doubt this is the end of it, quite the opposite, in fact. Do you really think the Yanks are going to leave it like this, I don't think so, do you?"

* * *

Leonard Cain walked in to the Situation Room of the White House and looked around at the staff assembled in front of him. The Vice President, all the Joint Chiefs of Staff, head of Homeland Security, Director of the CIA, and the Secretary of State were all there looking at him. They all wanted—and many demanded—a response to the attack on U.S. soil from Great Britain.

"I have been in contact with our assets in Britain and I have decided to respond with appropriate force to that what was executed here at home at NORAD. I have given the order to destroy the following three locations on mainland Britain. Firstly, the two nuclear reactors at PASTec would cause the radioactive contamination of the complex and thus rendering the time machine useless to them. Additionally, it would cause the deaths of many hundreds of people. Secondly, the destruction of their country's defence communication center, GCHQ. Finally, just so they know we're really pissed off with them, the attack will culminate in the destruction of Buckingham Palace—hopefully with some of the royals in the process. Any questions?"

* * *

Fenton rematerialized in a park about a quarter mile from the Geneva Hilton Hotel where he intended to stay. Again, he felt nauseous for a few minutes after time travel. He walked to the shopping mall on the way and changed some of his money into Swiss Francs at the bank there and then walked on to the Hilton.

After booking in and unpacking, he went down to the bar and ordered a Southern Comfort and lemonade with ice. He found himself a comfy chair by the window and stared out onto the neat, manicured lawn. Now he was here. He intended to stay in this time. He had to think how he would get a job and open bank accounts with no paperwork. How would he in the future get around meeting himself? Though all that could wait, tonight he had a date with his future ex-wife.

* * *

The British battle fleet anchored in the Solent had watched the U.S. carrier group weigh anchor and leave without a word. It was decided that the HMS Prince of Wales and two Type-45 escort destroyers and one Astute-class sub would follow the Americans back up the channel to the Atlantic and international waters. The remaining ships would return to their homeport of Portsmouth and dock in the naval dockyard. The remaining two submarines patrolled the waters of the English Channel to ensure no American sub stayed behind to cause trouble.

* * *

"What the hell is our carrier group doing? I ordered them to stay put in the English Channel. What the devil are they doing coming back? Why aren't they responding to communications?" said the President.

Admiral Cartwright had no answer. He had been trying to communicate with the strike group for hours but couldn't get a response. This was extremely unusual and worrying.

"Send some ships and planes to intercept them. Find out what the devil's going on."

* * *

Fenton booked a taxi for 6:40 P.M. to take him to Claire's apartment three miles away. Sitting in the taxi he found that he was getting butterflies in his stomach. How could he get butterflies, he thought, when he was married to her for years? He felt like a teenager going out on his first date and told himself to get a grip.

The taxi pulled up outside the address on the card at 1853 and found Claire waiting outside. She saw him in the back of the taxi and beamed a big smile and waved to him. She got in next to him and kissed him on the cheek.

"Hi, Fenty. You're early. You're showing promise. That's what I like."

"Promise?"

"Yes. Otherwise known as enthusiasm."

"Do you know of a nice restaurant around here? I don't know of any because I don't get out much normally."

Claire smiled and waved a finger at him and said, "You know of the old adage, 'all work and no play.'"

"Yes, and believe it or not, I'm actively working on that."

"Good." She turned her attention to the driver. "Café des Bains, please."

With that the taxi pulled into the traffic. "So, where are you staying?"

"The Hilton."

"They're obviously paying you too much."

Smiling back at her he said, "It's only temporary. I've not been here long and I've got to get a job."

"Oh, I thought you worked at CERN?"

"No, just visiting."

She raised her left eyebrow. "Visiting… a visitor with an unrestricted access identification badge with your name and picture on it?"

"Er…yes."

"Well, that's a new one for me!"

* * *

"Turn that bloody alarm off. I can't think with it going off in my ear," said Dylan.

"Okay, Dyl," replied Liz and walked over to the control alarm panel to enter the code.

"Silence, thank God, now get someone to turn off the main breakers. The time machine won't shut off again from my computer."

After thirty seconds, the circuit breakers were tripped, "Bollocks, the wormhole's still there, it appears to be running on its stored energy again."

"Er, Dyl, you're not going to believe this, but not only is the wormhole sustaining itself but the mouth is actually expanding. It's expanding beyond the time displacement area."

"What? Quick! Record its rate of expansion and clear the lab of all unnecessary personnel now!"

"Its now four inches beyond the displacement area. It's headed to the stair gantry" replied Liz.

Dylan wished now that the professor was here to help. The wormhole expansion that was occurring like this had never happened before and he could have done with his help. "Dylan, I'm registering negative energy within the wormhole and the strange thing is the negative energy is increasing?"

"What, but that's not possible. Unless... unless... no, this isn't possible."

"What is it?" replied Liz.

"Well, it is theoretically possible that there are naturally occurring wormholes in the universe that feed on negative energy. If there are, then our artificial one created here could be feeding off of this negative energy at the quantum level. If that is the case then, then..."

Then a look of horror went across his face. "If it's feeding at the quantum level, we have no way to stop it. As it feeds, it will get bigger and bigger."

"But I still don't understand, Dyl. We've shut the whole time machine down. What's feeding it without the machine's help?"

Dylan looked at the reading on his screens from the machine to the wormhole itself. He looked across at Liz with eyes wide with horror as realization dawned upon him. "I don't think we can stop it. It's taken on a life of its own. Unless there is a natural law in quantum physics that limits the size of wormholes at the quantum level, it will continue to grow and grow."

The impact of what he had just said showed on Liz's face. "You mean it will draw in matter from this space time?"

"Yes, and if we cannot shut it off, it will eventually swallow everything here, then the world and then beyond!!"

"Oh my God, what have we done?" cried Liz, with a look of horror in her eyes as her hand covered her mouth.

"Liz, look... look at the screen displaying the video from inside the time displacement area."

"My God, it's showing images of what has happened since the first time slip we did over five days ago."

"The wormhole appears to have remembered, so to speak, all the past events of the last five days and is repeating them in chronological order over and over at a vastly accelerated rate. If that's the case, then... then... we have inadvertently created a temporal causality loop."

* * *

Fenton sat across from Claire and watched her eat Black Forest cake. It was always her favorite sweet, especially when it had lashings of fresh cream poured over it as it did. He smiled. "You'll get fat eating that, you know"

"Bit of a charmer, you are. You certainly know how to impress a young girl on the first date. You sure you don't want any?"

"No thanks, I don't like sweet things. Now if they did a curry-flavored cake, then I might be tempted. Technically speaking, this is not our first date."

She looked curious. "Is it not? When was our first date then?"

"Which one did you want to know about?"

She ate another spoonful of cake. "Now you're confusing me. How can we have had more than one?"

Fenton remembered his first date all those years ago that still hadn't yet happened here in this time. It took him about a week to build up the courage to ask her for a date, although he had been working closely with her when she was his liaison assistant. If she had said no, he would have felt embarrassed and that would have made working with her uncomfortable. But he couldn't resist and, luckily, she said yes. So he took her for a hamburger and fries, which was all washed down with a can of Pepsi. Whoever said younger generations can't be romantic?

"Hello, you still in there? What are you thinking of, Fenty?"

"Oh… no, nothing really. Our first date was yesterday in the complex canteen. This is our second. I'm hoping there might be a third?"

"You order me another sweet martini and lemonade, and the answer might very well be yes," she said and beamed that big wide smile of hers again. He thought, Christ, it's a good thing he hadn't had any cake and cream because if he had had—with a smile like that beaming back at him—he was sure he would have dribbled cream all down his shirt.

* * *

As night fell, Harry was in Number 10 with the Prime Minister and Devon discussing what the response of the Americans might be and what response he was sure they would get, when his cellular phone rang in his breast pocket.

"Rocky? You got Rocky as your ring tune, Harry?" said Devon, grinning.

"Nothing wrong with that is there?" replied Harry going red faced as the Prime Minister sat looking at him with a slight smile and nodding his head gently from side to side.

"What? When did this start? What do you mean you can't shut it down? You're—what? Evacuating the PASTec complex? Let me speak to the professor. I can't? He's where? 2011? What the bloody hell is he doing there? What's going on down there? Look, hang on, we'll be over there in thirty minutes."

"Terry, can you get a helicopter for me here quick, I need to get to PASTec ASAP."

* * *

Fenton and Claire sat in the taxi holding hands, and looked out of the windows as the city passed by. When they pulled up to her apartment on Cours des Bastions, she turned to him and said smiling. "Would you like to come in for a coffee? My percolator makes a mean cup."

"Oh, go on then, you've forced my arm, if you insist." He paid the taxi driver and followed Claire into her first floor apartment.

The apartment was small but tastefully furnished with two, three-seater, red colored sofas around a large Moroccan style rug with a small mahogany coffee table placed on top. The rest of the furnishings were simple with little clutter. The walls were painted in a rich cream color except for the fireplace wall that was painted in a matching red. All this made the room appear bright and airy. Claire stood in the small but well equipped kitchenette making the coffee. While it was percolating, Claire turned around and flicked a few switches on a small control panel on the worktop. Soft music started to play from the speakers around the room.

"Who's this playing? It sounds familiar."

"'The Look of Love'. It's by a Sixties singer called Dusty Springfield."

Fenton stood at the large lounge window and pulling back the curtains looked out across the road at the trees that stood in the center of the road. The trees were full of leaves and many small birds were perched upon the branches all chirping a gentle evening song.

All the buildings in the road had that same neoclassical look about them. They were all in good condition, which gave the area a look of understated wealth and class.

The smell of coffee wafted across the room to his nostrils, and turning he saw her pouring out two cups.

"I suppose you don't take sugar, since you don't like sweet things?"

He smiled. "Three please, Claire."

"You're doing your best to confuse me tonight. By the way, I like the shirt. Who bought that for you?"

"How do you know that I didn't buy it myself?"

"Because it's stylish and it's something a younger person would choose. Though I'm not saying it doesn't suit you, because it does. So as I said, who got it for you?"

"Me mum!"

Claire walked across the room and handed a mug of coffee to him and said cheerfully, "Here you go, mummy's boy."

CHAPTER 7

Sunday, 1:07 A.M., Day 7

The Dauphin helicopter flew in low and went to land. Even though it was just after one in the morning, Harry could clearly make out the area of distortion around the main complex building. "My God, look at that, Devon. This is incredible!"

Devon had decided to go with Harry to the complex so she could make a full report to the Prime Minister by the morning.

The Chopper landed on the main lawn five hundred yards from the main complex. Both Harry and Devon got out and walked quickly to an office outbuilding well away from the main complex. As they approached the entrance, Dylan walked out of the building and strode up to them. He shook their hands quickly, then turned and went back into the building. Harry and Devon followed him into the building. They walked into a small meeting room just inside and to the left, where a few other laboratory technicians were already sitting. Some were drinking tea. All were strangely quiet and calm.

Dylan immediately briefed them on the events in the last few hours and about the rate of expansion. "Sweet Jesus, temporal causing hoop, did you say?" said Harry.

"No, temporal causality loop, also known as a predestination paradox."

"What's that mean in English, Dylan?"

"Right, well, basically, the time machine has in essence become live. It's feeding off of the negative energy that is everywhere around us at the sub-atomic—or quantum—level. As it feeds, it grows, and as the wormhole grows its captures the physical four-dimensional space-time that we all live in. As it captures this physical space-time, it seems to remember any event that happened in that four-dimensional space and runs those events over and over, repeating the same time again and again."

"So... so what we can do to stop it?" replied Harry.

Dylan looked straight at him with a hint of irritation on his face and said, "You don't seem to be grasping what I'm trying to tell you, Harry. We can't do anything, unless there is some law within quantum mechanics that we don't know about yet that limits the size of wormholes, this is the end of everything. Not just here, not just Britain, and not just the world, but also everything in the universe. Time will, in effect, stop in this timeline. The wormhole is growing at an exponential rate. We estimate that the world has less than twenty-four hours left before it is enveloped in the expanding wormhole. Then we will all live this last same week again and again for eternity."

Harry and Devon just stood there staring at Dylan. They were both grappling with the reality of what he had said. Neither found that they could say anything, but both thought the same thing. They were staring at the abyss. They realized they were looking at the end of time: time's end.

"We all need to leave this place right now, Harry," said Devon in a shaky voice.

Looking at Devon, Dylan shook his head, "Why? Where would you go? Britain will be swallowed up in the next few hours. Where then? Australia? That will be gone by the end of the day. The space station will be enveloped by early tomorrow morning, the Moon by tomorrow night, and the Solar System the end of this month and on and on accelerating across the universe at an ever increasing exponential rate."

Devon walked off to one side and stared out the window of the office into the darkness. She said quietly, to no one in particular, "The Bible said it took God six days to create the world, and it's just taken us six days to end it." She turned slowly and walked out of the building. An area of spatial distortion greeted her just a few feet away. As she stood there—staring at the end of time with a tear running down her right cheek—she let it swallow her up.

CHAPTER 8

Monday, 7:45 A.M., Day 1

The alarm clock buzzed in his ear, just as it did every morning. Professor Fenton Jones awoke clutching the pillow next to him. The feeling of loss peaked as he again realized that it had been a dream. Laying there naked, not bothering to turn the alarm off, he let it run the full minute before it turned off. Looking out of the bay window of his small country cottage, he watched the sun slowly rise above the Hampshire hills in the distance. He turned, looking at the empty space next to where he lay for a few moments reminiscing. He remembered her smell, her laugh, and her zest for life. He rose and as he walked to the bathroom he stood looking into the mirror at his thin five foot eight inch frame and partially thinning hair.

"Yep, same old Fenton, just another day," he said to himself.

EPILOGUE

Fenton opened his eyes and looked up at the white ceiling. He could hear her breathing slowly and gently next to him. He turned his head and looked at her face. Claire was laying on her right side facing him fast asleep. Her naked form was partly covered by the white satin sheet. He leaned over and breathed deeply and smelled that same sweet perfume she always wore. It brought back memories from all those years ago, in the future.

The aroma of coffee was still in the air from the percolator that was still on. Only now it was filled with the remnants of stewed coffee.

He hadn't intended for this to happen on their first date, but it just seemed right. Now that it had, he intended never to lose her again.

Lying there looking at her beautiful face, he decided he would go to the United Nations with his proposal of an international time machine project that he would lead and direct. He would ensure it was not to the detriment of his personal life. He would also be armed with this foreknowledge of the malfunctions and the mistakes of the alternate future program. He would ensure the time machine project would not be rushed, as previously happened. Besides, he couldn't go back to his time anyway because he'd already missed his twelve-hour extraction time limit.

It wasn't often, he thought, that you truly get a second chance in life. But he really had and nothing was going to come between them this time around...

The End, or is it?

Lightning Source UK Ltd.
Milton Keynes UK
UKOW04f2210121213

222944UK00001B/44/P